Holy Homicide

A JESSAMY WARD MYSTERY

PENELOPE CRESS, STEVE HIGGS

Contents

The Ghost of Reverend Weeks

'D on't fret so, I'm sure nothing is broken"

"Fret? I don't 'fret' - I merely express concern. It's a heavy box, and it sounded like something smashed."

"Nothing smashed; what do you have in here, anyway?"

I paused before answering.

"To be honest, I have absolutely no idea! Do you want a break? I have a shopping bag with tea and milk and other bits of life's essentials in the kitchen, and there's also an intriguing metal tin on the table. I think it is a gift from the parish secretary. My guess is that it contains cake!"

"Homemade?"

"Probably," I replied. Freya clapped her hands and dashed out towards the kitchen. "Thanks for helping me move in," I called out, following her down the hall corridor. The brightness of the winter sun blinded me briefly as I walked through the arched doorway. Once my eyes adjusted, I could see the full splendour of this slightly shabby but nevertheless impressive original Georgian kitchen with its flagstone floor, free-standing cupboard and ceramic sink stand. There were only a few nods to modernity, notably the electric lighting and an Aga cooker (that was going to take a bit of getting used to). With a little tender loving care, this would be a stunning place to enjoy a breakfast coffee.

I found Freya wrestling with the cake tin by the oak table.

"My pleasure! Anything to help my favourite aunt. Boy, this is tight... do you have a knife?"

I went over to the painted dresser beside the Aga. I noticed how forlorn it looked without any plates on its shelves. It would be fun trawling the boot fairs and second-hand shops to find some interesting pieces.

"Strangely enough," I said, yanking at one of the dresser's stiff wooden drawers, "I noticed there was some cutlery in here earlier. Not sure there's a knife though, it might be all spoons."

I rummaged through the drawer's contents until my hand found an overly ornate fish knife.

"That'll do." Freya grabbed the fish knife and made short work of the tin lid. There, as promised, was a beautiful round cake covered in white royal icing and the words 'Welcome Vicar!' delicately piped in blue icing. "What's inside? I'm guessing a Victoria sponge, but could be chocolate, I suppose?"

"Far more likely to be a fruitcake, given the icing. You don't usually put icing on a chocolate cake, or do you? Now, I need to find a kettle, or a saucepan and mugs. I really hate moving."

Not having had my own parish before, I was a little short of my own belongings except for more personal items. It was a relief to learn that the vicarage was 'fully equipped'. I just had to find where everything lived. A few minutes and several cupboard door slams later, we had two mint green 'Beryl' ware cups filled with steaming milky tea and two matching side plates adorned with thick slices of dense, alcohol-soaked, fruit cake. Each slice wrapped in pale mustard marzipan with a half-inch layer of icing.

I was delighted to have found a cupboard filled with this classic vintage crockery design from the 1930s, though there is probably a similar set in every school and church hall across the country. It was making my return to this island parish feel even more real.

Freya rocked back on her chair and balanced her trainers on the edge of the packing box under the table.

"Four feet on the floor, Missy! Your Mum will kill me if you fall back and break your skull open on these kitchen tiles."

"Aunt Jess, you worry too much. I am perfectly in control. Though I might be a little off-balance after eating this cake, I think someone has been a little overzealous with the sherry."

There is a particular peculiarity in my family line for each successive generation to have one family of three girls. My mother was one of three girls, she went on to have three daughters, and now I have three nieces: Clara, Phoebe and my favourite Freya. Freya has a playful spirit, full of wonder at the world around her - carefree, confident, and vibrant. In total contrast, her older sister Clara was a serious child who has grown into a serious adult. Not surprising really, as my flighty sister Zuzu (or Susannah, as my parents named her), left much of the 'adulting' to little Clara from the moment she could walk. Zuzu loved adventure. She loved men. She especially loved adventurous men, and adventurous men rarely have time for small children, least of all three little girls.

Maybe that is why Clara dyes her hair a dark auburn, I thought as I sipped my tea, to cover up the natural sandy locks she inherited from her mother. Blondes may have more fun, but Clara has a serious need to be taken seriously. Her mother definitely had fun. If I am being honest, I was incredibly jealous of my sister's 'joie de vivre' growing up, and that love of life is what I like most about Freya. Poor Clara is more like me. Reliable, dependable, and predictable. Although, at least Clara has the nerve to dye her hair, I am too afraid to even do that. The shots of grey I now sport are the only highlights of colour my mousy strands have known. Freya's hair, of course, is as luminous as she is: Freya has a natural copper glow.

"Let's get back to work before you fall asleep on me then," I said as I carried the cups and saucers over to the Belfast sink. I glanced out at my new garden, admiring the frosty, subdued tones of the herbaceous border. I thought of the time and love the previous tenant, Reverend Colin Weeks, had put into it. Though I hardly knew him, I felt sad that he could not see the results of all his hard work. The reverend had been in St. Gregory's Hospice, on the mainland, for nearly six months. After his death, someone had emptied the vicarage of all his humble belongings months before they offered me the post, though I doubt he had left much behind. As someone who could kill a plant simply by looking at it, I decided that one of my first tasks would be to find a green-fingered volunteer to help me maintain Reverend Week's horticultural legacy, or there would be nothing left to show for the forty years he served this parish.

My personal memories of Reverend Weeks are sketchy at best. My mother had taken my sisters and me away from the island to the mainland after my father died. I was only thirteen. Reverend Weeks had been the parish priest for about four years when we left, but I doubt I would have known him much better if we had stayed. My family were not great churchgoers. In fact, most of my relatives still struggle to understand my calling to the priesthood. The Anglican Church and my ancestors have not always seen eye to eye.

Ageing Hippies and Cats

I remembered well the conversation that brought me back to the Island.

"Reverend Jessamy Ward!" Only Bishop Marshall, my mother and cold callers, ever called me Jessamy.

"I think it's time for you to have your own parish. The vicar on the Isle of Wesberrey passed away a few months ago. Terrible end, pancreatic cancer, most unpleasant. Anyway, God has welcomed him home and his happy departure leaves a vacancy that, well, if I am honest, no one else is overly keen to take on." The bishop had the most unusual, sonorous voice that made everything he said sound like a Gregorian chant. "I understand you know that godless outpost. Still have family there and such like. It will be a challenge. Mainly ageing hippies, crusty old fishermen and eccentric misfits, but I am sure you will do your best."

"And cats, you forgot the colony of feral cats," I said.

"Ah yes, the cats! Colin used to complain that they would keep him awake all night fighting in the graveyard."

"I'm not sure this is the right posting for me, your Grace. I do have family there, but I haven't seen much of them over the years. My mother took us away when I was a teenager, and I have no desire to return there. I was hoping for an inner-city parish where I can bring God's love to troubled youths, isolated pensioners, the lost and the lonely. As for the cats... I'm allergic!"

"This is a great opportunity, Jessamy. You can bring God's love to a community which has turned its back on him. They are truly lost. God is calling you. You are the only man, I mean, woman, for the job."

I knew at that moment that I had no choice. I would be returning to Wesberrey.

"And what about the cat allergy?" I asked.

"Take some antihistamines!"

Talking of Ageing Hippies

"So, where is my favourite niece?" My Aunt Cynthia knew exactly where I was. I was right in front of her. "Jess! Let me look at you." With these words, she grabbed me firmly by the arms and spun me around to get a full 360-degree view. "That dog collar suits you in a 'why in all that is sacred would you want to be a vicar,' kind of way."

"Thank you for the compliment, I think? Welcome to my new home." I slipped out of her clutches and stepped back, motioning her with an arm in the direction of the kitchen. "Would you like a cup of tea? I believe there is still some sherry-soaked fruit cake left unless Freya has finished it behind my back? Freya! Come and meet your great-aunt Cynthia."

Freya called back from one of the reception rooms towards the front of the house, her voice getting louder as she moved towards us.

"Isn't Cynthia the new age witchy one? Is she here? Mum says she's literally away with the fairies, talks to them at the bottom of her garden and everything... Oh! Hello Great-Aunt! I'm Freya, Zuzu's daughter. Nice to meet you."

"Wonderful to meet you too, Great-Niece Freya, daughter of Zuzu." Cynthia replied like a character from a Tolkien trilogy, seemingly unruffled by Freya's talk of fairies and witches. "How is your mother? She will return here soon. We need to find you both a little house nearby. I will ask around..."

"Sorry..." said Freya, obviously a little concerned about her great-aunt's confusion. "You misunderstand. Wonderful as Wesberrey is, I am not staying. I have to get back to uni, and my mother has no plans to return. She is busy with her latest project in Brazil, and I doubt she will even have time to visit over the next few months. But I am sure now Aunt Jess is living here, my mother will pop over as soon as humanly possible."

Cynthia smiled a knowing smile. Her long slim finger stroked a loose curl of reddish-gold hair back in place behind Freya's ear. Then she cupped Freya's face gently with both hands.

"I understand."

She paused.

"I will look for a house presently."

Freya and I exchanged looks of complete bewilderment. My mother had told me about Aunt Cynthia and her conviction that she was blessed with the gift of second sight. Our family can trace its ancestry back on the Isle of Wesberrey to the seventeenth century. Family folklore asserts that the female line goes back through to the time of the Druids, when a pagan cult dedicated to a fertility goddess trinity had a settlement on the site where the parish church now stands. Cynthia believes herself to be the latest in a long and venerable line of 'wise women' who have maintained the secrets of the Goddess, passing down the fecund deity's rites and rituals from aunt to niece for generations.

The 'aunt to niece' bit is critical. According to the myth, every generation will produce a family of three sisters. One of these sisters will become the 'mother' and one will become the 'godmother' or priestess. Her role is to protect the Goddess and intercede with her on behalf of all the women who seek her help. The 'godmother' does not have children herself, but one of her sisters will have three daughters, one of whom will take on the role of 'godmother' at the appointed time.

For my mother's generation, the three sisters were Cynthia, my aunt Pamela who also still lived on the island, and my mother, Beverley. In mine, I have two sisters: Zuzu - Freya's mum and Rosie. Both Pamela and Rosie have sons. Both Cynthia and I are childless. I believe it's all nonsense, but there is a spooky cross-generational pattern.

"And darling, please," Cynthia sighed. "Please, oh please, stop calling me Great-Aunt, ugh, makes me sound like I'm a hundred and three! Save that for your Great-Aunt Pam, if you ever see her. It's almost impossible these days to get her and Byron away from their programmes. Heaven help us if she misses an episode of 'Above Stairs' or the 'Great British Bake Off'! Look, just call me Cindy. Everyone else does. Well, they call me plenty of other names too, but let's not go there... so, Freya, I hear you are studying Anthropology at university, which will come in very useful when you take over from Jess. Of course, that is a long way off yet. Plenty of years left in me."

And with a swish of her cashmere shawl over her left shoulder, Aunt Cynthia, sorry Cindy, sauntered off into the kitchen.

"Now, where is this cake you were talking about?"

First Impressions

F ortunately, I have few possessions, so moving into the vicarage was a relatively straightforward process. I do, though, have a fine collection of Murano glass fish, which I have picked up from Christmas bazaars, summer fetes and numerous jumble sales over the years. They are not to everyone's taste, but I was looking forward to proudly displaying them in my new home. My new home. My home. My own home. For the first time in my five decades on this planet, I would not have to share that home. The thought filled me with joy and a pretty sizable slice of anxiety. But it's not like I will ever be lonely. My new parishioners would soon make themselves known and there were my estranged family members to reconnect with.

With Cindy and Freya bonding over unpacking the last couple of boxes and, no doubt, questioning my taste in objet d'art, I ventured out into the fresh evening air to chair my first Wesberrey Parochial Church Council meeting, aka St. Bridget's PCC. All the council members had dropped in to welcome me during the day, and I had already met most of them during an earlier visit with the diocesan archdeacon just after Christmas. I took this warm interest as a positive sign. Even though I had the full support of the Bishop and Archdeacon, and the churchwardens had appeared to be happy with their choice of vicar-in-chief, until my official 'Service of Welcome' (or collation, installation and induction, to use the full ecclesiastical terminology) where the official transfer of rights to the benefice are handed over to me, the lay patrons of the parish could change their minds. This would leave me without a job and my colourful fish without a home.

Unsurprisingly then, given the importance of this first meeting, I admit I was feeling a little queasy, and it had nothing to do with the alcoholic cake. Fears of potential homelessness aside, this meeting was crucial in setting the right tone for my future ministry. I needed to establish order, control, and authority.

I stood outside the ancient door of the vestry hall, took a deep breath, and pushed down on the ornate handle with a firm, determined grip.

Though I had a strong hold on the handle, the solid oak door with its cast iron hinges had the upper hand. I rattled the handle up and down, but the door would not budge. Getting frustrated I barged against the wood with my shoulder, pushing it open with a sudden jolt that sent me flying into the echoing chamber.

"N'ermind Vicar, that door is always a bit of a beast, you'll soon learn the 'ang of it!"

The broad tones of Phil Vickers, verger, and landlord of the Cat and Fiddle pub down on Harbour Parade, boomed across the cavernous room. So much for my assertive power entrance!

"Here you go Vicar, take my seat. I've been warming it up for you. Nothing worse than a cold behind when there's important business to discuss."

I turned to the second voice to see Barbara Graham, parish secretary and baker of the sherry fruit cake, stepping away from the chair she occupied at the head of a trestle table.

"Thank you, Barbara. That is very thoughtful of you, but there's no need to warm my seat up for me. I've enough padding down there to mitigate even the frostiest of chairs."

I laughed. They laughed. All is well.

"Okay then," I said, looking down the table at the assembled PCC members. "I am delighted to see you all here tonight and promise you I'm not in any hurry to make any sweeping changes to how things are done at St. Bridget's. My understanding is that a sub-committee of the council meets weekly to discuss general matters. That would be you, Barbara, me and Phil, the churchwardens, of course." I waved my hand towards two elderly gentlemen sat at the end of the table. "And the full council gets together once a month to sort out the big events and issues like budgets, fundraising and so on. Is that correct?"

"Spot on Vicar," Phil replied. "Under Reverend Weeks, God rest his soul, Barbara and I pretty much worked out all the day-to-day stuff. Babs is an absolute treasure. There is nothing she doesn't know about this church and its parishioners."

"Oh Phil, you are making me blush!" protested Barbara. "You know this old place wouldn't function without you and your magic toolkit. There's not a latch or a screw that man there hasn't nailed, greased, or painted back into life. The old abbey would be in ruins without him."

Barbara and Phil were obviously the 'go to' couple if I wanted to get any information or to get anything done. And quite the couple they were, too. I was too fresh to know for sure if they had been, were ever, or had plans to be an actual 'couple', but the chemistry between them was palpable. I hazarded they were probably both in their mid to late fifties. Phil sported a full beard and wore his grey hair in a rather fetching low-hanging ponytail. There was a roguish air about him, enhanced by an ever-present mischievous glint in his green eyes. Barbara was a buoyant lady who obviously enjoyed eating the cakes she made. She was no stranger to the sherry bottle, as I knew already. She was no stranger to the peroxide bottle, either. Her short blonde hair may once have been natural, but her slate black eyebrows suggested otherwise.

Sitting to one side of Phil on the long side of the trestle table were the churchwardens, two balding ex-public servants, who, now they were sitting together, reminded me of Waldorf and Statler from the Muppets. The official role of a churchwarden is to support the vicar and maintain the parish services during their absence. The previous incumbent had been dead for over six months, in a hospice for three months before that, and probably could not officiate fully for several months before entering the hospice. I imagined the churchwardens would be a little wary of a new vicar. Waldorf, sorry Ernest Woodward, was the first to speak.

"Reverend Ward, I understand from Bishop Marshall that you are related to one of the older families on the island. I believe I knew your father, Michael. God rest his soul. I recall he was in the year above me at school. Different times, different times. Of course, there was a war on. Changed us all. Yet still, for him to marry one of the Bailey girls, well that *was* a surprise!"

Tom Jennings, or Statler, clapped his hands in excitement.

"Oh, but Michael was an extremely handsome man, those eyes. How they pierced out through his dark fringe. Almost black his hair was, with a blue tint in the light. It was no small wonder your mother cast her spell on him. Once he showed an interest, she would have been a fool to let him get away."

"I never noticed his eyes," Ernest said pointedly. "But he came from a very conservative family, traditional, upstanding members of the congregation. It broke his grandmother's heart. She died when she heard the news. So tragic!"

"With all due respect, Mr. Woodward, Mr. Jennings, my father loved my mother with no need for magic tricks or potions." I spurted out, quite shocked at how emotionally I was responding.

I had naively believed any resistance to my appointment would come from the reluctance to release their influence over the parish or the introduction of a female priest. I did not, for a minute, think that the biggest issue would be my maternal family's reputation as witches.

"Seriously, you two are worse than a couple of old fishwives, and being an old fishwife, I should know! Old Grandma Ward was the best part of a hundred years old when her only grandson, Michael, married. She died of old age, short and simple. No magic, no curses, no nothing. Reverend Ward, I am deeply sorry for any offence these village idiots have caused you. They are genuinely good men, if a bit too prone to idle gossip."

The elderly woman behind these words and the withering stare aimed firmly at Ernest and Tom was Rosemary Reynolds, Treasurer, organist, and longest-serving member of St. Bridget's PCC.

"No offence taken, Mrs. Reynolds, thank you. I understand that I have ties to this community that are woven into the fabric of the place, even to the foundation of the convent that they built this abbey upon. I trust I will have the full council's support as I serve the current community going forward."

They all nodded. *That's a relief. I can unpack the fish.*

"Let's talk about more exciting things," ventured a quiet voice from the far corner of the table. "We have to discuss the preparations for the bishop's visit next month. For your Service of Welcome. It is truly a sign from Our Good Lord above that it is to fall on the feast of St. Bridget... Now, about the decoration of the vicarage, you know Reverend Weeks was very frugal. He only ever spent money on the garden. Barbara and I did our best to give it a good clean, but it is really stuck in a time warp. I am sure that Reverend Ward has plenty of ideas for home furnishings, but, well, there is a little money in the pot for some paint, maybe even some wallpaper. It's very on trend to use paper right now, unless you prefer a minimalist look. I was thinking about some nice florals. I have a mood board here for the morning room, quite my favourite room in the house."

For a quiet mouse in the corner, there appeared to be no stopping Rachel Smith now she had our attention. She had popped by the Vicarage earlier, as had everyone else, but curiously didn't say a word beyond her name and that she was really pleased to finally meet me. Rachel now dived under the table and returned with an A4 cork board, covered in wallpaper samples and fabric swatches, and placed it in the centre. Adjusting her tortoiseshell glasses and pushing the straggling ends of her jet-black hair behind her ears, a blushing Rachel carefully explained her English garden theme. Soft lilac wisteria petals, grey satin trellis and highlights of leaf green that would 'bring the summer inside all year round'. Everyone stood up and gathered around; there was a gentle mumble of 'oohs' and 'aahs'.

When everyone had given their comments about the proposed design, we settled back into our seats to discuss the bishop's visit. Barbara and Rachel fussed around organising cups of tea and coffee for everyone, and plates of white bread sandwiches with vague, grey-brown fillings followed.

"Some are meat paste, though I think these ones are tuna." Rachel said as she passed me a plate. I picked one up to sniff. It smelt slightly fishy so, hoping it was indeed tuna, I took a nibble. It was. With a nice fresh slice of cucumber in the centre.

"These are lovely," I said. "Who is the cook?"

"That would be young Rachel. I stick to cakes usually. By the way, I hope you got the one I left you at the Vicarage. My fruit cake is quite the talk of the Island," said a very proud parish secretary. "I used less sherry than usual, didn't want to make you drunk before your first meeting!"

"Very considerate, and quite delicious, thank you Barbara," I replied. "And thank you all for such a warm welcome. I am sure we will work very well together. By the way, Rachel, I really like your plans for the morning room. Do you want to pop up tomorrow to help me measure up?"

Rachel puffed up her pigeon chest and could not have smiled more proudly if she had won the Turner Prize for her designs.

"Thanks, but no need Vicar, I have all the measurements already... and, well, actually..." Rachel took advantage of the empty seat next to me, sat down and with a nervous giggle added, "I have already ordered the paper. It should be here on the ferry tomorrow. I have asked Robert Barrett, the postman, to collect it from the ferry and bring it up here when it arrives. Unless you would prefer that I hold it at the shop until you have unpacked?"

The Smiths ran the island's only bookshop, the imaginatively named 'Island Books'. The same family had run Island Books for generations. This was very common on Wesberrey. I could remember looking into the bookshop on the town square as a girl. A dusty, dark place with shelves upon shelves of hardback books and yellow film covering the windows to protect the volumes inside from the glare of the afternoon sun. Something about Rachel told me that the shop probably still looked the same. It would be interesting to find out.

"Yes, if you could keep them at the shop. I could pop in to get them later when I am more settled. Thank you."

With the business of the meeting closed, as the members made their way out into the main church, Rosemary grabbed my arm. She pulled me back away from the others and whispered in my ear.

"Be careful of Rachel. That poor girl looks for love in all the wrong places. All her life she has cared for that mother of hers, without so much as a kind look in return. I said she should have put her in a home years ago. Such a waste, cooped up in that house, or in that mausoleum of a shop with dead poets for company - it's enough to drive anyone insane! I can't say any more, Vicar. Just don't let her get too close. You can't give her what she craves. I doubt anyone can. So very sad."

Rosemary walked off, shaking her bowed head.

And so 'endeth' my first meeting.

A Good Night's Sleep

Freya had made herself at home in my absence. Evidence of basic meal preparation remained around the stove and sink area. *Beans on toast? Classy!* There was also a handwritten note.

Had too much cake.

Feeling unwell. Gone to bed.

See you in the morning.

F x

Though I adore my niece, I relished this unexpected opportunity for a hasty cheese sandwich partnered with a delicious mug of cocoa and a few quiet moments to myself. The gentle pit-a-pat of the rain on the windows soon soothed away the stresses of the day. *I think I've made a good impression.* Time will tell.

I had brought Rachel's mood board with me from the church hall. The amount of work that she had put into it was flattering. I guess there's not much to do in Wesberrey on a cold winter's night. *It's so quiet here.* I was used to the driving hum of city traffic. All life blurring into a never-ending syncopation. Only the sirens of the emergency services punctuate the night air, and in time, even they become like white noise. *This will take some getting used to.*

My head dropped and woke me up. *I must have nodded off.* Time to test out my new bed. I added my mug to the great unwashed in the sink basin and double-checked all the locks before ascending the stairs. You can take a girl out of the city, but the city in the girl remains scared of intruders in the dark.

My room was freezing. Someone, probably Barbara, had opened the windows to let in some air, but it was January, on the south coast of England, and that air was biting cold. I changed into my pyjamas at record speed and threw myself under the feather duvet. A few grateful words to the Big Boss in the sky, and I was ready for a good night of blissful sleep.

Except that is not what happened.

Maybe it was the cheese sandwich, but all night I tossed and turned like a freshly made salad. Every time I fell back asleep, it would be to the same dream. Or should I say nightmare?

Moments after I closed my eyes, my subconscious mind would transport me to a tiny bedroom. At first, everything looks normal. Against the back wall stands a cast iron bed frame, smothered in cushions and plush toys. The room then swirls around me, and a massive vortex opens in the centre of the room — sucking the bed, the cushions, and the cuddly companions into an inky hole. I grab onto a door handle, fighting the gravitational pull into the unknown. I lose my grip and water floods in through the now open door. A wave lifts me up towards the ceiling and then spits me out onto the harbour wall. I land in Market Square, wearing only my nightclothes, a few yards from the ferry.

A voice from behind calls my name. I turn to see the faint whisper of a young woman walking toward me. Her face shimmers as round and pale as the moon above. Black tendrils float around her head. She is the gathering storm that brought me here. I want to pull away but am mesmerised by her eyes, which, like toothpaste squeezed from the tube, bulge from their sockets. Terror holds my feet to the spot.

She mouths the words "Help me." and then tugs at the scarf around her neck. A long low ooooooooo whistles from her lips, grey-blue as the North Sea on the far side of the island. They twitch for a moment and then stop. I wake up in a cold sweat.

When my alarm went off at seven o'clock, I must have visited this hellscape half a dozen times. *Note to self: No cheese after dark.*

A Trip to the Market

"Hmm, that Rachel has a good eye for design," said Freya as she stood in the morning room holding the floral mood board up in one hand and a slice of buttered toast in the other. "Though you have to admit it's creepy that she had already ordered the paper. What if you hadn't liked it?"

"I suppose we would have sent it back. I think she likes a project. From what Rosemary said last night, I think Rachel leads quite a quiet, possibly lonely, life."

"Well, as long as she lets you choose how you decorate the rest of the house, though perhaps that's not such a great idea given your bizarre obsession with glass fish. Where are you going to put them all?"

"I was thinking of getting a glass cabinet or two. You know the ones with mirror shelves and built-in lights, so the colours reflect off the fish? I'm just not sure where to put them."

"What about the shed at the back of the garden?"

"Cheeky! I guess you don't want to come with me to Market Square to check out the shops then. I thought we could go to the Cat and Fiddle for lunch."

"Sounds thrilling!" I detected a slight note of sarcasm in Freya's response, but she quickly brightened. "Talking about cats, when I went to put the cardboard boxes into the recycling bin last night, I noticed a small stack of tinned cat food by the side gate. Any idea who left them there?"

"Not a clue," I replied. "But I think I know why. This island is historically famous for three things: the legend of the triple goddess, witches, and its colony of feral cats."

"Of course, you can't have witches without their cats. What are they called... familiars!" Freya laughed. "What with Cindy's sixth sense nonsense last night, creepy bookshop owners, feral cats, and your glass fish, I feel I have fallen into a parallel universe. Let's go to the shops, a nice normal activity."

"Rachel isn't creepy. I really like her, but I'm not sure there is anything normal about shopping in Market Square. However, I'll let you judge that for yourself," I said as I grabbed my coat.

Tom and Ernest

T here are two routes from the Vicarage to Market Square and, as the January morning air was exceptionally crisp, we took the fastest route, namely the Wesberrey Cliff Railway. The Cliff Railway is a funicular railway that runs vertically between Cliff View and Harbour Parade. Though a little creaky, this old lady still provided the most efficient way to move people and goods between the two main centres on the island. Resplendent in her burgundy and gold painted iron livery, this beautiful example of Victorian engineering is quite the tourist attraction during the summer season. Throughout the winter she provides warm and dry transportation to and from the harbour and commercial town centre at sea level and the abbey and surrounding municipal buildings: the village hall, school, and cottage hospital, up on the hillside. As there are no cars allowed onto the Island, the railway provides an essential service to the local people. The two cabins only hold around eight people each, but fortunately, alternate on a journey that takes only three minutes from beginning to end, and the views are stunning.

I was a little surprised to see Tom Jennings at the 'Cliff' ticket office.

"Good morning, Vicar, and how are you this extremely fine morning? And your lovely young niece, so nice of you to help your aunt settle in. All that unpacking must be quite the chore. Heading to Island Books? I hear your wallpaper arrived on the first ferry this morning. Seventeen rolls... I trust that will be enough. Rachel is very precise. I am sure she has calculated what is required exactly, though I do hope she has allowed for matching. Some of those blooms were quite large."

"I'm sure we can order more if required, Mr. Jennings. I didn't know you manned the railway alongside your duties as a churchwarden. You are a man of many talents," I said.

It occurred to me I was going to have to get used to everyone knowing about my business in such a small community. From the wallpaper to my trips into town, everything would be public knowledge.

"Well, it's good to keep busy. The devil makes work for idle hands and all that. You will find Mr. Woodward below at Harbour station. Keeps him out of mischief."

"Really? I look forward to seeing him again. How much for two return tickets?"

"Oh, no charge for you, Vicar. How else are you supposed to get down there to tend your flock?" He smiled.

"Thank you, Mr. Jennings, that is very kind. Will you still be here when we come back up this afternoon?" I asked.

"Oh, no it will be Ernest then. We like to switch over after lunch. Just helps to break up the day. By the way, we close for an hour at twelve-thirty, otherwise, I would faint clear away without something to eat. I will see you at the bottom this afternoon. Enjoy the trip, Vicar. You too Miss Ward."

***

"Miss Ward!" Freya crashed down on the wooden slatted seat to the front of the cabin. "No one has ever called me Miss Ward, makes me sound like a primary school teacher. 'Good morning children. Good morning, Miss Ward' — awful! The views, though, are amazing!" With that, she pulled out her phone and took pictures of the harbour and coastline beneath. "It's such a clear day. Look, you can see the mainland. I wonder how many people in the high-rises over there look out to the land that time forgot and realise just how barking everyone is here."

"It's not quite the land that time forgot," I said. "Granted, we are currently in a Victorian railway cabin descending slowly to a ferry port, which is the only real way on and off the island. The narrow roads and antiquated bylaws mean that there are no cars, which takes a bit of getting used to, I admit. The same families have lived here for generations. Everyone is related to everyone else. And all and sundry know your business, and let's not forget the cats, but... there are telephones and satellite TV and Wi-Fi. The twenty-first century is getting through, and to be honest I like not having cars. Evil polluting things. The Island is quaint, traditional, welcoming. Many people dream of living somewhere like this."

"Yes, in their nightmares! Aunt Jess, are you sure you are going to be happy here? Maybe Grandma was right to leave all those years ago?" The cabin stopped with a thud.

"Good morning, Reverend Ward! I trust this morning finds you well. I hear your wallpaper has arrived," said a very earnest Mr. Woodward as he pulled back the sliding metal door to the cabin. "Ah, Miss Ward, good to see you. Hope you both have a very pleasant day."

I thanked Ernest warmly and ushered Freya out onto Harbour Parade, assuring her I was very content with my new position and this unexpected return to my past. I was feeling weirdly defensive about everything. *Perhaps due to lack of sleep.* This new world would take a lot of acclimatising to, but, as we dodged a clowder of cats, awaiting the spoils of the fishing boats, (what a funny word clowder is...) I silently hoped I would soon develop a personal immunity to the Island and its more peculiar human and furry inhabitants. I was determined to make this posting a success. *Note to self: Stop by the chemist to stock up on antihistamines.*

Passing the Cat and Fiddle, on the right-hand corner of Harbour Parade as we turned into Market Square, I bumped into my verger, Phil Vickers, washing the pub's windows. He looked like a middle-aged Jack Frost in his pale blue check shirt, and stone-washed denim, all drenched with water from his exertions.

"Good morning, Phil, you look frozen, be careful not to catch your death of cold! I have just seen Mr. Jennings and Mr. Woodward. I didn't realise they ran the Cliff Railway."

"Old Tom and Ernest? Well, it's so convenient for 'em as they live in the white 'ouse next to the railway on Cliff View. You're neighbours, Vicar. When they both retired, they were the natural choice to keep that thing runnin'. It would 'ave probably closed without 'em volunteerin' as they do. In the winter there's not enough commercial usage to make it viable to run a full service. It barely breaks even during the tourist season. That railway costs more to maintain than the parish earns from it. I do my bit to keep the machinery workin' but any replacement parts must be custom made."

"Tom and Ernest live together? In the White House? I had no idea!" I exclaimed, perhaps showing a little too much surprise.

Phil continued washing the windows and appeared to not immediately pick up my reaction. "Tom and Ernest? They've been a couple for years. Decades if truth be told. The entire island knew. You can't hide anything around 'ere. Though they only moved in with each other a few years ago. Such a shame to 'ave to hide your feelings away like that. Both 'ad important jobs on the mainland. I guess they didn't feel safe to express, well —" He suddenly stopped talking. Wringing out the wet cloth in his hands, he turned to me. "Oh my, Vicar, sorry! Do you disapprove? I mean, they are good men, they do so much for the church, for the community. It would kill 'em if you, I mean..." Phil looked at me with the wide-eyed alarm of someone who had just betrayed their best friend's deepest secret.

"Phil," I reached out my hand and rubbed his arm to comfort him. "I believe in God's love. Full stop. And I believe we are all his children. I do not judge. That's not my place. Love comes in many forms. It is the single greatest gift we have from our Father in heaven. It unites us all. We are all brothers and sisters in Christ. One family. As Jesus said, let he who is without sin, and all that jazz."

Phil threw down the cloth and pulled me in for a big, soggy, bear of a hug. "You're a good woman, Vicar. We were all worried that the bishop would send some fire and brimstone preacher 'ere to put us all straight. We don't need an outsider telling us 'ow to live our lives."

"But I am not an outsider Phil, remember? I am one of you."

He nodded and pulled away. I resisted the urge to rub my compressed arm. It would have ruined the moment.

Market Square

The buildings in Market Square all date from the late eighteenth and early nineteenth centuries and were built upon the original medieval foundations. The impressive Portland stone Guildhall, with its large Venetian windows and imposing blue enamelled clock face, sits elegantly above the original wooden trading hall in the centre of the square. Farmers and artisans have bought and sold their goods here for over nine centuries. It is a romantic backdrop to a bustling market that still draws a wide interest from the surrounding mainland towns and villages every Tuesday and Thursday. Even on this bracing Thursday morning, the market was heaving with people.

The stalls interlacing the portico columns of the hall were overflowing with selections of fresh produce, flower bouquets, craft goods, and homemade preserves. From deep within the hall floated a jangly melody I eventually recognised as 'Knees Up Mother Brown'. As we followed the music through to the centre of the stalls, Freya spotted Cindy talking to a dapper young man standing next to an impressive barrel organ. This stunning wooden instrument featured some quite exquisite marquetry depicting various types of birds, fruits, and flowers, and had a dozen or more inset brass pipes. It was being cranked into life by a twenty-something male dressed in suitable Victorian garb, complete with velvet waistcoat, paisley neckerchief and houndstooth flat cap. From her sudden giddy behaviour, I think Freya was more taken with the organ grinder's warm brown eyes, and how his soft brown curls tickled the edge of his collarless shirt, than with his mastery of concert hall tunes. *Not that I noticed, he's half my age.*

"Freya, darling, what serendipity! I was just telling Dominic about my beautiful great-niece and here you are. Gorgeous Dominic is an art student with a particular interest in the Pre-Raphaelites, especially Dante Gabriel Rossetti, who also had a bit of a thing for redheads."

Dominic blushed and gallantly held out his hand to Freya. "Very pleased to meet you. Cindy has been telling me all about you. Cindy is an artist too. Have you seen her work? Quite breath-taking. Your great-aunt has an exceptional eye for beauty."

He took Freya's hand and bowed his head to kiss it. I have never known Freya to be speechless until now. I stepped in to save her. "Dominic, lovely to meet you. I am the new vicar, Jessamy Ward. I have just moved into the Vicarage on Cliff View. Do you live locally?"

Dominic released my niece's hand gently and straightened himself up to take mine. "Welcome Reverend Ward, no, not local. I am studying at nearby Stourchester University. I volunteered to play this organ for the Christmas market and, well, Cindy offered to let me stay at her house and I just can't seem to leave. The island is so captivating. Everyone here has a unique aura. Take Cindy here. I have learnt so much from her. Wesberrey offers an artist so many muses. Do you paint?" Dominic looked inquiringly at Freya as if a no from her would have broken his heart in two.

"I dabble," Freya replied nonchalantly. This was the first I knew about her dabbling. Though I suspected she would have suddenly developed a lifelong interest in stamp collecting if he had asked her.

"So, er, Dominic, you are staying with my great-aunt? You should both pop over for dinner. Do you plan on staying long? I have to head back to uni myself soon. I should really be studying, but I was intrigued by my aunt coming back to the Island and offered to help her move in." My niece stroked her throat as she spoke. *A common matching signal, I understand.* "I've never been here before. Though our family tree goes way back. It is wonderful, isn't it? Well, what I have seen so far. I love it."

Love it? Only a few minutes ago, Freya was saying this place was the stuff of nightmares. How quickly a girl's head can be turned by a pair of handsome eyes.

"Darlings! I have a marvellous idea. Dominic can show you around. I have an old scooter in my garage and two helmets. What are you doing tomorrow? The forecast is for another glorious day. You could go around the Island in a few hours. I will make you both a picnic lunch."

Cindy was turning into quite the matchmaker. It would be impossible for either party to refuse.

"That sounds lovely." Both replied in unison.

The spell had been cast.

Island Books

There was no point in trying to prise Freya away from the attractions of the market, so I left her with Cindy and strict instructions to meet me back at the Cat and Fiddle for lunch. I carried on across the square to pop in to see Rachel in Island Books. As I suspected very little had changed since I was a child. Though the yellow film was gone, the bookshop looked just as dark and unwelcoming as I remembered. A bell jingled above the half-glazed wooden door as I pushed the handle and called inside.

"Is that you Reverend Ward? Robert hasn't got here with your wallpaper yet, but I hear it's arrived. He will probably make me his last stop. He usually does."

Rachel emerged out of the darkness carrying a pile of leather-bound books, which she placed on the corner edge of a battered oak desk that was already groaning under the weight of other similarly bound volumes. "Can I make you a cup of tea? I am afraid I don't do coffee. Mother hates the stuff. She says it leaves a nasty aftertaste, which I suppose is true. I only tried it once, by mistake. It was at a church 'Bring and Buy' sale. I thought it was tea. Picked up the wrong cup. I won't be doing that again in a hurry. Anyway, as I said, Robert should be here soon."

I thought I detected a slight flush on her cheek when she mentioned Robert's name. However, Rachel was obviously flustered. She kept moving piles of paper from table to shelf and back again, rearranging the cups and saucers on the tray repeatedly, and talking a mile a minute. Though she was animated when we last met, this 'busy-ness' was different from the excited woman I had seen the night before. Several times she took off her glasses to clean them on the cotton gauze scarf around her neck, obviously agitated about something.

"Sorry, Reverend Ward, you must think me a terrible mess. I thought computers meant we would have less paper, not more. I just seem to have more and more paperwork, even when I do most of the shop's business online. How did we cope before the internet? I'd be lost without my laptop. Mother doesn't allow us to have a television, but I can stream movies and box sets anytime and, as long as I keep the volume down, she is none the wiser. Sometimes I use the subtitles and play Mozart in the background, saves me a lot of grief — is that very wicked? Right now, where was I? Ah yes, tea! How do you take it?"

"Milk, no sugar, thank you. Rachel, Rosemary told me that your mother is housebound. That must be quite the strain on you, what with managing the shop as well, and all you do for the PCC."

"That meddling busybody. Did she tell you she thinks I should put Mother in a home? A home! It would kill her! My Mother hates other people. Loathes interacting with anyone. The very idea of dumping her in one of those homes, living out her days in one of those clinical community rooms. They are always green and cream, aren't they, with prints of flowers or country lanes. Like there's only one interior designer for every care home in the land. I can't imagine Mother sat in a winged-backed chair, looking out over a boring manicured lawn with daytime television blaring out in the background. No, absolutely not. And don't even try to convince me, Reverend."

"Rachel, please, I wasn't going to suggest any such thing. I was just wondering if there was anything I could do to help you. Perhaps I could look in on your mother during the day, or... what about giving you a night off so that you can go out, relax a bit?"

"Thank you. I appreciate your offer, but I am fine. Let's have tea. I have some bourbons somewhere." Rachel frantically opened and closed drawers. "If you don't like them, I think I have a pack of Garibaldis in the back. Squashed fly biscuits we used to call them. It must be strange coming back here after all these years. When did you leave?"

"1980, I was thirteen."

Rachel smiled. I wasn't sure if she was anxious or excited. There was a strange look in her eyes that belied her positive demeanour. She was hard to read, but something was clearly making her edgy.

"Of course, the year I was born. I guess a lot has changed since then. Not this shop, though. I doubt this will ever change. Do you remember it?"

I remembered this shop and being too scared to go inside. I also remembered an intimidating lady, with jet black hair and vivid blue eyeshadow. She was always standing outside when we passed. She had the most enormous beehive hairstyle I had ever seen. Her epic hairdo was held in place with an extra wide purple hair band that forced her more animated locks to seek alternate escape routes. She reminded me of Medusa from the film Jason and the Argonauts, and that film sent me running behind the sofa — especially the scene where the skeletons come to life! Although, for some reason, I don't think my fear of animated heads with snakes was why my mother used to push me and my sisters past the shop so quickly. 'Medusa' always shouted something at us as we passed, but I cannot remember what she said. Could this harridan have been Rachel's mother? If it was, then with the clear exception of her stunning hair colour, Rachel must take after her father.

"Rachel, I was wondering if you might be free to help me tomorrow to start the decorating. Freya will be off to university again in a couple of days and, well, now the wallpaper and paint are on their way. Strike while the iron is hot and all that."

Rachel mumbled something but seemed distracted by whatever she was looking for out of the shop window. Clearly, she was waiting for Robert, the island's postman. The imminent arrival of my wallpaper rolls may have explained her current state of anticipation but was more likely about seeing the man who was delivering them.

"I haven't had the pleasure of meeting Mr Barrett yet. Is he local?" I asked.

"No, Robert doesn't live on Wesberrey. He gets the ferry over from the mainland with the mail. He's taking his time this morning. Must have been delayed. Would you like another cup of tea, Reverend?" Before I could answer, Rachel jumped up, smoothed down her skirt and disappeared into the back of the shop with my half-drunk cup of tea.

Moments later the bell rang, the door pushed open, and a bear of a man backed into the shop and turned slowly towards me. "Rachel, Rachel, you naughty little minx. Where are you hiding? Daddy's got a special parcel for you — Oh! Didn't see you there."

I stood up to greet a very rattled middle-aged man wearing a scarlet Royal Mail uniform, a walrus moustache, and a nervous look.

"You must be Robert." I held out my hand and then realised that his hands were full of wallpaper rolls. "Here, let me take these off you. I think they're mine anyway. I am the new vicar, Jess Ward."

"Oh yes, of course. Hold on, there are more outside. I'll just get them."

The nightmare scenario of struggling back up the hill to the vicarage with seventeen rolls of wallpaper skidded across my mind. "Actually, Robert, would you mind taking them up to the Vicarage? If they are already in your van. I think Rachel is helping me decorate tomorrow. Sorry to mess you around."

"Yes, yes, of course. Whose stupid idea was it to bring them here anyway? I mean, I could have just taken them straight there this morning. That was the original plan, but hey, let's not think about my inconvenience! I start my round at the top of the island, you see, and work my way down, and it would have been a lot easier to have offloaded these first thing. There's not much room in the Ape for bulky items."

As there are no cars allowed on Wesberrey, the closest thing to a van is the Piaggio Ape. A small three-wheeler built on a scooter base. Many businesses use them on the island and adopt a tractor for larger goods.

"I'll just take these back then." He growled as he collected the rolls he had just brought in and shuffled towards the door.

"Let me open that for you!" I ran across to help open the door, as Robert's arms were full.

"Thank you. Vicar. How very thoughtful of you." He glared at me as he pushed past, muttering something about 'bloody women' as he left.

At that point, Rachel reappeared. "Sorry Reverend, did I hear Robert's voice?" she asked. "I got distracted by an order that had just come through on the computer, whilst I was making the tea. Very rude of me to leave you here all alone. Is he coming back?"

Rachel looked anxious. Perhaps she thought I had snuffed out his ardour. Bumping into a member of the clergy can do that to a man. I think Robert expected to have his fire put out today, but not by me.

"I believe so," I replied. "He is just taking the rolls he brought in back to the van. I asked if he could take them up to the Vicarage. I think I upset him. But I thought if you are going to help me decorate tomorrow, and if he has transport, it would be easier."

"Oh, I am sure he isn't upset. No need to be sorry, Reverend. He just gets a little frustrated when people change plans on him. You know, take him for granted... mess him around... only natural, I suppose. Everyone wants to feel appreciated. I do tell him to relax more. Getting so uptight isn't good for his blood pressure."

"Yes, of course. And I really appreciate it and your help too. So, will I see you tomorrow, about nine am?" I said, realising that Rachel had not actually agreed to come up to help me yet.

The bell went again, and a calmer Robert walked back in.

"Nine o'clock in the morning... tomorrow? Yes, that's fine Reverend, I look forward to it." Rachel looked directly at Robert even though she was speaking to me.

"Oh, and I almost forgot. Rachel, I don't suppose you have a copy of Julian of Norwich's 'Revelation of Divine Love'? I seem to have mislaid my copy, and I wanted to use it to help write my sermon for Sunday."

Rachel nodded. "I think there's a copy at home. I could bring it up with me in the morning?" The look on her face told me that was my cue to leave the two of them alone.

"That would be wonderful, thank you. And Mr Barrett, thank you too. I know I'm being a right pain. Lovely to meet you. If it helps, the wallpaper and paint can wait 'til the morning too?"

"I will pop it up this afternoon, else I'd have to take it back home with me, then to the sorting office, then back here again…" A small vein was ticking on Robert's left temple as he spoke.

It was definitely my time to go.

"Ah, yes, right, silly me. Well, no rush. I'm meeting my aunt and niece for lunch. Just put the rolls by the back door."

Leaving the heated conversation behind, I welcomed the cooling air on my face as I emerged back onto the market and headed off to the Cat and Fiddle.

Thank Goodness it's Friday!

Lunch with my aunt and niece was interesting. The whole pub was alive with the sound of gossip. There was a mysterious stranger in town, and it wasn't me. It seems that after less than a week I was now considered a native, though I suppose I was originally, whereas this 'man in black' was an outsider. No one knew who he was, or why he was here, but several of the locals had seen him walking around the town late at night. There were often tourists or tradespeople from the mainland, but they usually returned home on the last scheduled ferry. It was rare for anyone to stay this time of year, so the rooms that were available in the pub, and numerous cottages and caravans along the coastline, usually lay empty. Phil assured the lunchtime regulars that he would ask the ferryman, Bob McGuire, if he knew the identity of this enigmatic visitor. The ferry was the main way on or off the island. Though it would be possible that the stranger had come in on a private boat, the consensus of those gathered was that this was extremely unlikely, and that Bob would know anyway, because Bob knows everything. Phil had made a solemn pledge to all assembled that he would update everyone at lunch the next day.

It was now the next day and, buttoning on the collar to my shirt, I reflected on how good it felt to be part of a community and privy to the latest gossip. I was as keen to find out about the 'man in black' as everyone else, but such discoveries would have to wait until later. Robert had kept his word and delivered the wallpaper and paint the previous afternoon. Freya and I had spent the evening preparing the morning room so that Rachel and I could get cracking on the decorating as soon as she arrived. Fortunately, I had found some old t-shirts that I could throw over my normal vicar's garb to paint in, and there were some rubber gloves in the kitchen.

Far more attractively dressed, Freya had left, just after sunrise, with Dominic on the back of a sage green death trap that my aunt assured me was totally legal on the roads of Wesberrey. The ancient Vespa had seen better days, but that did not dent my niece's desire to set off with her handsome companion for a romantic tour of the island. I doubted I would see her again before dark and, whilst I waited for Rachel, I took advantage of the solitude to catch up on some paperwork.

Barbara was proving to be a very efficient parish secretary. She had neatly stacked all my correspondence on a rather striking, and beautifully polished, regency mahogany desk with a green leather top. My guess was that this desk was as old as the Vicarage itself. If it could talk, I am sure it would have an amazing collection of tales to tell. All of life would have passed over it: births, deaths, and marriages; sins and scandal; penitence and perversion. Now it boasted four paper hills, each with a yellow post-it note advising what lay beneath:

- *Urgent - act now!*

- *Important, but not a priority (read when you have some time)*

- *You probably don't need to read these,* and

- *Recycling*

Thinking that I would ease myself in with the 'Recycling' pile, I took a quick look through the contents on my way to the kitchen, dropped the papers in the bin, and went back to my office via the kettle. *Well, I have had a busy day already.* Having grabbed a fresh cup of roasted bean juice, I set to work on the 'Urgent - act now!' pile. The first document was a set of instructions on how to use the antiquated computer on the desk, with an apology that it was so slow. I used the step-by-step guide to log on and access my emails at rev.j.ward@stbridgetsabbey.org.uk. I also had access to the general office email. There was only one email in the rev.j.ward account and that was from Barbara congratulating me on getting this far. *I suspect Reverend Weeks had been less computer savvy.* The office account had a few unread emails that had come in overnight. Most were spam, but one was from Rachel Smith, sent around eight o'clock that morning. It read:

Not feeling very well. Can't come today. Rachel.

Finding Hugo

I hate to admit it, but I was quite relieved to hear that Rachel was unwell. Not that I would wish ill health on anyone, but because I was enjoying the peace of my new home. I worked through the 'Urgent' pile as quickly as possible and then went for a walk to explore the church grounds.

The Vicarage stands on the foundations of the former abbey dormitory, once occupied by around eighty medieval nuns. The convent was founded in the seventh century. All the nuns were local women who tended to the sick and destitute in the infirmary, which now forms part of the church. The infirmary hall was built, as was the custom of the day, to give the patients full view of the chancel and the priest conducting mass on the high altar. The nuns worshipped in an adjoining chapel. This layout can still be seen in the design of the twelfth-century Norman abbey that replaced the original church which was destroyed by the Vikings. An interesting feature that remains from the original building is an image of a goddess with three wheat stalks, an ancient fertility symbol, on one of the columns of the Nun's chapel. There is also the image of the pagan god known as the Green Man in a triangular stone above the Priest's Door in the Lady Chapel. Allegedly, the Green Man stands on a direct ley line between two of the three wells that form the Wesberrey Triangle.

Now, according to Cindy, just like the Green Man carving, my return to St. Bridget's was a sign. Exactly what it was a sign of she was a little vague about, but she believed I was to succeed her as the 'godmother' and she tipped Freya to take over from me. Though Cindy did also say it could be either of Freya's sisters, Clara or Phoebe, as none of them had children yet. It appears that the main qualifications for this prized role are to be a) one of three sisters and b) to have no children. I pointed out that Saint Edith, the medieval queen who had founded the convent, was one of three sisters, but she had had a son who became king when her husband died. I had been doing my research. Cindy brushed me off, saying, "No one said Edith was the 'godmother'. She was a saint!" To which I had replied that it was all coincidence and nonsense. Though walking around the church and looking at the pagan images carved into the stonework, it was obviously nonsense that had a long tradition here.

On the opposite side of the abbey sits the Wesberrey Cottage Hospital, which currently has about twenty beds for local people to convalesce in. Rather ominously, the church graveyard runs along the back. I would be visiting the hospital tomorrow, so decided that today I would do a tour of the headstones. It's always sobering to see the names and ages of all those who have gone before. They too had once loved and cried, had dreams and fears. The graveyard was rarely used today. Most people chose cremations, and often family plots were full. It was easier to be buried on the mainland. I knew Mum had cremated my father's body. Instead of interring his bones into the ground, we had scattered his ashes from the cliffs nearby.

To add a dramatic effect to that particular thought, a bitter wind suddenly whistled through the stones. I could swear that I heard the cries of the dead swirling around me. A shiver ran down my spine.

"Jess, stop being stupid," I said, as if talking to myself was not stupid enough. "It's just your super vivid imagination. First, I'm having bad dreams and now I can hear the spirits of the dead talking to me. I watch too many horror movies."

In the centre of the graveyard stands the Somerstone family mausoleum. This enormous marble tomb has four Doric columns, and an impressive terracotta slate roof, and is ridiculously hard to ignore. This architectural marvel competes for prominence on the skyline with three key municipal buildings. The austere Victorian red brick Cottage Hospital, the Georgian Vicarage with its elegant lines and ordered sash windows, and the chiselled stone of the Norman Abbey. The tomb's exterior walls are ornamented with exuberant nymphs and fauns — more pagan influences on church property. And the family name 'Somerstone', is etched out in gold lettering about a foot high above the entrance.

I was considering the inappropriateness and pointlessness of this extravagant structure when I got an eerie feeling I was being watched. In the wind, the cries of the dead grew louder. I turned around. Very slowly. Creeping towards me were a dozen or more cats!

The cries of the dead in the howling wind had simply been the mewing calls of hungry felines. The poor things were probably starving. Despite Freya alerting me to the deposit of cat food by the bins at the side of the house, neither one of us had come up here to feed these sad creatures. They drifted towards me, obviously expecting that I had something to give them, curling around my legs and nipping at my shoes.

"Sorry guys..." I called out as I ran back towards the Vicarage, "I'll be back in a minute, I promise."

Just inside the back door, there was a pile of old baking trays. I was not sure what they were used for before, but I knew what they would be used for now. I grabbed one of the empty packing crates and loaded it up with the baking trays, some plastic cartons that Freya and I had been using before discovering the bowls and plates and carried it all out to the bin where I added the tins of donated cat food.

Most of the cats had stayed in the graveyard, but I noticed one had followed me back. He appeared different from the rest, who were mostly short-haired tabby cats, or tortoiseshell varieties. Probably a Persian mix, this striking boy wore his black fur long and his eyes glowed like burning coals.

Remembering my cat allergy, I dashed back into the kitchen to take some tablets. My new friend followed and jumped onto the chair, then the table and sat there. Waiting. His red eyes softening to pale amber in the kitchen light.

"Okay, okay, I'll feed you first." I opened one of the smaller tins and emptied the fishy contents into a shallow saucer from the green tea set we had found on my first day. It was gone before I could rinse out the tin for the recycling. "Do you want some more? I guess you're famished."

I opened another tin and watched as he licked up the last morsels and then his lips. Patting him gently on the head, I tried to coax him off the table. "C'mon cat, I need to take the food up to your friends and I can't leave you here."

He would not budge. I tried picking him up, but he kept wriggling free like a black slinky toy. I tried pretending to walk away, in the hopes that he would follow. He did not move.

"Fine. Stay."

I sneezed.

"Check the place for mice whilst I'm gone."

I walked out knowing that I had just been adopted by a cat and smiled.

"I think I'll call you Hugo," I said as I closed the door. "You remind me of an equally stubborn ex-boyfriend!"

The Harridan's Den

O nly a day had passed, but I suspected that Hugo (the cat, not the ex-boyfriend) was a stray and not one of the feral cat colonies. The main differences being his friendly nature and obvious desire to stay indoors, preferably on the top of the small bookcase next to the radiator in my office. Freya, safely returned from her perilous journey around the island, had taken to him straight away, and he to her. Perhaps he could sense that I was allergic, as he generally kept his distance from me unless I had food. Fortunately, the antihistamines seemed to be working. Though I wasn't sure it was a great strategy to make them a daily habit. I would ask the doctor when I visited the Cottage Hospital later that morning.

Outside, the weather had turned, and a thick fog rose from the sea to cover the cliffs. I could hear the warning bells of the ferry in the distance and a gentle foghorn sounded from the lighthouse on the far side of the island. This morning I was really grateful for the funicular railway to take me safely down to the town centre. Ernest was on duty at the Cliff station, and he greeted me with his usual propriety. Tom's greeting was as cheerful as I expected it to be when I reached the bottom. I made a mental note to invite them around for dinner one evening when I was more settled. It would be the neighbourly thing to do.

Tom was full of talk about the 'man in black'. Bob McGuire had brought him to the island late one evening, on a specially chartered ferry crossing. It transpired that Bob often transported people to and from the mainland out of hours, for a price. Bob said that he took the booking from Tristan Somerstone-Wright, grandson of the current Lord Somerstone, and son of actress and socialite Arabella Stone (her stage name, short for Somerstone, obviously) and her financier husband Gordon Wright. From Tom, I learnt all there was to know about Arabella Stone. Back in the yuppie days of the eighties and early nineties, Arabella was known as an 'It Girl' and was quite the party animal before settling down with Mr Wright. The constant partying had taken its toll on her looks, and she was now a bit of a recluse, breeding micro-pigs on her farm at Bridewell Manor. Arabella's husband, Gordon, spent most of his time in London and Tristan was at boarding school. Neither were resident on the island. The 'man in black' therefore, must be visiting Arabella, he surmised. I imagined Tom had spoken about nothing else all evening and poor Ernest was relishing the break offered by his duties at the top of the railway.

I had several errands to run. One of the many quaint things about island life, but one that I was struggling to get used to, was the lack of a supermarket. There was no one-stop shop on Wesberrey. This was an attractive quirk to day trippers who enjoyed meandering around the little shops and market stalls, but it was a complete pain when you needed to get lots of different things in a hurry. In terms of square footage, Market Square was probably on par with the larger out of town supermarkets on the mainland, and the variety of goods available was comprehensive enough for most daily needs. What ate away at my precious time was having to queue up to pay for each item or items separately. I love people, it's my job, and Market Square on a Saturday morning is a great place to meet my new parishioners, but I needed to complete my shopping and get back to the Cottage Hospital before my appointment at midday, and it was already close to ten thirty.

Errand one was completed with ninja-like stealth. The trip to the chemist was a quick in-and-out raid, stopping only to pay for my tablets and a speedy 'How are you doing? Fine thanks and you? Grand, that'll be £3.50, great, thank you and goodbye!'

Next was the cat litter tray.

As I walked across the square to 'Bits and Bobs', the general gardening and hardware store, I noticed Island Books was closed. *Rachel must still be unwell.* I thought I should pop by after my visit to the hospital but realised that I didn't know where Rachel lived.

"How much for the litter tray?" I asked a bespectacled youth behind the cashier's desk.

"Erm... I'm not sure, hold on a sec, I'll go ask me Dad"

And like magic, Harry Potter's double vanished behind a brown curtain and a balding man with a hangdog look and egg stains on his vest emerged in his place.

"Can I help you, Vicar? My name is Stan. Stanley Matthews. My father was a huge football fan and couldn't resist. S'pose it could be worse... he might have been into turkeys!" This was obviously a joke, but Stan realised I needed more explanation. "He could have called me Bernard! As in Bernard Matthews, you know... like, as in Bernard Matthews's Norfolk Turkeys. C'mon you must remember 'Bootiful, really bootiful'... No?"

I continued to look blank. He shook his head.

"Stan, it's lovely to meet you. I'm Jess Ward. I seem to have adopted a cat and need a few bits. By the way, have you seen Rachel Smith? Her shop isn't open."

"Now you come to mention it, no, I haven't." Stan rubbed his sausage fingers over his stubbled chin. "The shop was closed all day yesterday as well. Very unusual, she's always open. Except for when she pops back to her home to make lunch for her mum... though, for the love of me, I can't think why she bothers to open at all. No one ever goes in there these days. Does anyone read anymore?"

"I think most of her orders are online. Do you happen to know where she lives? I said I would pop by to visit her mother one day."

"Visit that old soak? She won't have a clue you're even there! My advice would be to steer well clear. Though I suppose you God-worrying types think you can save her," he said, pointing at my collar. "Wasting your time there, Vicar. That one sold her soul for a pint years ago. But, if you insist, you will find her on Love Lane, leading off the back of the hospital, next to the graveyard. Number Twenty-four, I think. Anyway, you'll know it from the overgrown rose bushes in the front and the broken fence. You can't miss it."

I paid for the tray and a few catnip goodies and then headed back to the railway. If I was quick, I could nip in to see how Rachel was before my visit to the hospital. The fog had lifted, and the sun was shining brightly as I ascended the cliff side. I had to admit, the more I heard of Rachel's mother, the less enthusiastic I was about meeting her, but I believe everyone can find peace and salvation. After all, that was my job.

***

Twenty-four Love Lane sounds like a very romantic address, and it probably would make a cosy retreat with a little tender loving care. The weather-worn garden fences were bowing with the weight of the overgrown rose bushes that pressed against them, and their scratchy thorns caught at my coat as I tried to push through the small clearing by the wooden gate. The path up to the house was slippery with green moss. Along the edge of the path, such as it was, were barren cement troughs with protruding twigs I imagine had once been heather or hebe plants. I rang the doorbell and waited. A television was on inside. *Someone must be in.* I rang again and knocked, just to be sure. I knocked again with all the force I could muster, and the door pushed open.

"Hello! Rachel? Mrs Smith? Is there anyone home? Only me, Reverend Ward. Just checking you are alright."

I could only hear the television. It sounded like a crime drama. There was dramatic orchestral music playing and someone screaming. I ventured further inside. The small hall led straight on to the kitchenette at the back. A shadow dashed past at the far end.

"Hello? Rachel? Is that you?"

There was a crash!

"Rachel... are you ok?"

I edged closer to the kitchen door. My heart was in my mouth. Something was wrong. Something was very wrong.

"Rachel... please, I didn't mean to scare you."

A furry ginger streaked past me and out the front door.

"Oh, my! Get a grip, it's only a cat!" I leaned against the kitchen door frame to catch my breath.

"Go away! Go AWAY!"

The cry came from upstairs. This time, I knew it was not from the television.

"Rachel? Mrs Smith?"

I leapt up the stairs to the landing and listened. Sobs carried into the hall from the room to my right. I took a breath and gently opened the door. Nothing could have prepared me for what I saw next.

"Go away! Rachel! Rachel! Where are you? Rachel!"

A very distressed elderly woman, I assumed to be Rachel's mother, was sitting on a commode in the middle of her bedroom. The television I had heard was actually a radio set placed in front of a mirror on an oak chest of drawers to my right. Of course, Rachel had said they didn't have a television. A tray with the mouldy remains of a meal half-eaten was resting on the unmade bed. Mrs Smith had been here for some time.

"Mrs Smith, please... can you tell me where Rachel is?" My first instinct was to comfort the old woman, but I feared that something may have happened to Rachel, and she might need help. "I will be right back, I promise, Mrs Smith... Okay? I just need to find your daughter."

I went into the other bedroom. Rachel was lying stomach down on the bed with her gauze scarf tied tightly around her neck. Her pale face stared at me with bloodshot eyes through the tortoiseshell frames of her glasses, her lips blue and swollen.

She was dead.

My dream!

I knelt beside her and offered a simple prayer. Her lifeless eyes glared into my soul. "Rachel, I'm so sorry. You tried to tell me."

Jessamy Ward, listen to yourself. What utter nonsense. Go get some help!

An Inspector Calls

I t was not a new thing for me to see a dead body. In my job, I had ministered to the sick and dying many times, but this was different. This was murder. I needed to call the police, but I panicked. Instead, I ran to the hospital.

Running is not an activity I do a lot, and I arrived at the Cottage Hospital almost in need of an ambulance myself. Bent over, as I tried to catch enough breath to explain to Martha (the name pinned to the maroon uniform with the soft West Indian accent) that I needed the phone, a voice called out from the adjoining hallway.

"Jess Ward! As I live and breathe. They said it was you. I didn't believe them. Jess a vicar! No way, no way on this earth. And here you are, dog collar and everything. You're a bit early, but no worries."

I turned slowly, my bosom heaving as I continued to pant out my words.

"Sam?"

Samantha had been my best friend at school before my family moved to the mainland. We wrote to each other for a few years afterwards. Though we stayed pen pals for a while, without social media, it was harder to keep in touch back then. She had hardly changed. A few wrinkles around her deep-set hazel eyes and a slightly looser jawline suggested Sam was no longer the thirteen-year-old girl I remembered, but she was still as tall and as slim as before. Sam had always worn glasses; however, the stylish designer frames she was wearing now were a huge improvement on her former blue plastic NHS spectacles.

"Do you work here?"

"Work here! I'm the boss. Who would have thought it, eh? You, parish priest of Wesberrey and me, Clinical Director of the Cottage Hospital. You look a bit flushed — what's wrong? Here, take a seat."

"Sam, I must call the police. Rachel Smith is dead. She's been murdered!"

Maybe it was the dog collar, maybe it was my panicked state, but Sam didn't need to be told twice. She told Martha to call PC Taylor immediately and get him up here as soon as possible. She also arranged for the Wesberrey ambulance, well it's more like a tuk-tuk, to go the hundred yards to Twenty-four Love Lane and bring Mrs Smith to the hospital; with strict instructions not to touch anything else before the police arrived.

"Perhaps they could take photos of the room and how they find Mrs Smith before they move her?" I suggested. "Just in case it helps the police later on?"

"Great idea," Sam replied. "Guys, do as Jess suggests, minimum disturbance, okay? But we can't leave the poor woman there any longer."

Twenty minutes later Mrs Smith was being cared for on one of the wards and PC Taylor had cordoned off the house to prevent any further contamination of the scene whilst he waited for a senior officer to come over from the mainland. Sam took me into her office for a much-needed cup of tea.

"So, Reverend Ward. You never married then? Or are you still using your maiden name? I would have thought being a vicar you would be more traditional... and what on earth led you to become a priest?"

"And what on earth made you become a, what was it, Clinical Director?"

"Touché. Well, let's say I discovered I had a calling to help others."

"Well, let's say I had a calling to help others too," I replied. "And, no, I never married. You?"

"Oh, only twice, so far," Sam smiled. "I am back on the market again, as they say. But seriously, I remember you wanted to be a singer or something."

"Actress. I wanted to be an actress. I also wanted to marry Starsky."

"Ah yes, well I preferred Hutch"

"Or Erik Estrada,"

"Mark Hamill!"

"I remember you had a thing for Leif Garrett as well. Though I would have settled for Donny Osmond."

"Settled! You should be so lucky!"

We both laughed. It was a wonderful surprise to be with Sam again. We instantly reconnected and all our yesterdays melted away.

"I did try to be an actress, went to drama school in London and everything. I worked in a lot of community theatre stuff and then I had my big break. A small part in a West End play. On the way to my first rehearsal, a car swerved onto the pavement and hit me. I ended up in theatre but not the one I expected. They recast my part and I discovered the church. Well, that's the abridged version. Anyway, eventually, I realised what a blessing that accident had been. I became a vicar and, well, here I am back in Wesberrey, drinking tea with my old best friend. All meant to be."

"Meant to be indeed." Sam raised her cup of tea as if making a toast. "To friends reunited!"

"To friends reunited!"

There was a gentle knock on the office door.

"Sorry to disturb yer Dr Hawthorne, but Inspector Lovington is here to talk to the reverend."

51

"Thank you, Martha. Send him in, would you? Jess, I will leave you, if that's okay, and see how Mrs Smith is getting on," Sam said as she walked towards the door.

"Doctor Hawthorne? Doctor! I'm sorry, I assumed you were like the matron, or something."

I felt so embarrassed. Sam hugged me so tightly I thought I would break.

"It's so good to have you back, Jess. We are going to have so much fun. And behave yourself with the dishy inspector," she said, with a pantomime wink. "He has Donny Osmond's eyes. I'll be back. See you later."

The dishy inspector? I checked my appearance in the reflection of one of my friend's medical certificates hanging on the wall by the door. How had I not noticed that before? Sam had studied at King's College, London, no less. In fact, the entire wall was full of framed medical certificates. Very impressive.

"Reverend Ward? Pleased to meet you. I am Inspector Lovington of the Stourchester Constabulary. I understand you found Rachel Smith's body. Are you able to answer a few questions?"

The Stuff that Dreams are made of

I immediately understood why Sam had referred to him as dishy. Though his eyes were a lighter shade of brown than the puppy love crooner, I could see the resemblance. Inspector Lovington oozed vintage charm as if he had just walked out of a Bogart movie, except he looked more like Errol Flynn. He sported a stylish beige gabardine trench coat over a flint grey tweed suit. A fedora was the only thing missing from the classic detective look. The coat appeared to be an authentic Burberry. The stitching and details were exquisite. It must have cost the best part of a thousand pounds. I wondered how he afforded it on a policeman's salary.

Now, I would be the first to say that I usually preferred a clean-shaven face on a man, but, as he spoke, I found myself strangely drawn to how his fine pencil moustache etched across his upper lip.

"So, Reverend Ward, I understand you found the victim. May I ask what you were doing at the property?"

"Oh, please call me Jessamy or Jess. Yes, well, Rachel was to help with my wallpaper. I needed to get a cat litter tray, so Stanley Matthews suggested I go to Twenty-four Love

Lane. It was the radio, not a television, and there she was, obviously strangled." Words were crashing out of my mouth before my brain had a chance to check them.

"Erm... Okay..." He smiled, running the finger of his left hand around the inside of his shirt collar. The bemused look on his face confirmed he had obviously not understood a word I had just said. "Perhaps you could slow down a bit. I can't write that fast and I don't want to miss any important details."

"I am sorry Inspector, let me start again." This time I let my brain run first and the words fell out in a more logical fashion.

I did much better the second time around recounting why I was visiting Rachel's house and how I found her body noting all the salient details in a calm and logical fashion. And all that despite noticing midstream that the Inspector's eyes contained dazzling flecks of gold. I even held it together when he stood to leave, and the fluorescent light cast a halo over the tawny highlights of his slicked-back hair. I also remained remarkably unfazed as he shook my hand and thanked me for my time. I was a total professional. I only turned into a huge mushy lump of giggling girliness once he had left the room.

***

"So, what do you think of Inspector Loveliness?" Sam asked as she kicked off her work heels over the edge of the morning room armchair she had swung herself into a few minutes earlier. Sam had decided that I needed a 'girly night in' after the drama of the day and had popped in after her shift had ended with a perky bottle of Pinot Grigio gifted by a grateful patient at Christmas. "Be careful. I hear that he's as fresh and as fruity as this wine."

"I suppose he has a certain... appeal?" I replied.

"Appeal? The man is a veritable babe magnet!"

"Babe magnet! Is that a medical term for Adonis?" I sighed.

"See! I knew it! I knew you would fall for his GQ charm. You haven't changed a bit!" Sam laughed and bent across to massage her stockinged feet. "Oh Jess, it's so good to have you back home. It's been too long."

Feeling guilty about swooning over the police inspector called in to investigate the murder of one of my parishioners, I changed the subject.

"So, what brought you back to Wesberrey and the Cottage Hospital at that? Your certificates tell me you were carving out quite the career for yourself in London."

"The end of marriage number two. He was a surgeon at St. Thomas's. They say surgeons have a 'God complex'. Well Mister Justin Hawthorne, FRCS, thought his demi-god status entitled him to roger every student nurse in the hospital stupid enough to let him. Poor creatures. He always told them, get this, he always told them they were helping him keep a steady hand by... I mean... really! And they would fall for it. Christ! I used to fall for it! Sorry, I shouldn't blaspheme. Didn't mean to offend you, sorry."

"Sam, I am not that easily offended. You're speaking with truth and raw emotion. It's okay to use passionate prose. You know, you're the second person to worry that they have offended me. Honestly, my job has taken me to some of the roughest council estates in the country. I have seen and heard far worse, believe me. Here, have some more wine."

I poured Sam another glass and walked over to the trestle table Freya and I had brought in the day before from the vestry to use for pasting the wallpaper. The seventeen unopened rolls of floral wallpaper Rachel had chosen stood in a box against the wall. I wondered if Rachel hadn't been unwell and had come here as planned yesterday, would she still be alive?

"Who would want to murder Rachel Smith? It must have been an intruder. She was supposed to come here to help me decorate this room. You know, she picked the wallpaper, did all the measuring, even ordered it before I arrived. She was supposed to come here to help yesterday morning, but I got an email to say she was ill. Sam, do you think whoever murdered her thought the house would be empty? Or only her bedridden mother would be there? Instead, they found Rachel home from work. She rarely closed the shop. No one would have expected her to be there. And then panicked? Strangled her with the nearest thing to hand. Her own scarf. Then fled, leaving the front door open and Mrs Smith stuck on her commode. Poor woman."

"That sounds possible to me, just one question – what were they looking for at Rachel's house? She didn't have much. Island Books couldn't have made much money. I doubt she has a secret stash of jewels hidden under the mattress!"

Sam scrambled her legs around to the front of the chair and, with both feet firmly placed on the floor, leant forward holding the wine glass in both hands. "Unless she has discovered a rare manuscript hidden underneath all those dusty tomes, or perhaps someone's long-lost diary and she was blackmailing them, and they decided not to pay anymore or...."

"Or, someone has an overexcited imagination," I said. "It was probably just an opportunist thief who overreacted."

At that moment Freya came bounding through the door, followed closely behind by Dominic carrying a slightly soggy Hugo. "We found this chap outside in the rain. A quick once over with the hairdryer should do the trick!" Hugo jumped out of Dominic's arms and ran straight back out towards the kitchen.

"I don't think he likes hairdryers." Freya giggled. "I'll get his supper... er... do you want to help me open the can?" She smiled at Dominic, who graciously bowed at me and Sam before taking Freya's outstretched hand and following her out of the room.

Sam's gaze followed Dominic's exit.

"Oh, if only I was ten years younger."

"More like thirty!"

"Maybe I should think about a younger model for husband number three."

"Yup, I can see how a pair of strong legs would be good to help push you around in your bath chair. But keep your mitts off young Dominic. He's Freya's."

"So, Freya is your daughter?" Sam asked, "You said you never married."

"No, my niece. She was helping me move in before heading back to uni, though I have hardly seen her since she met Dominic. It was only two days ago, but things are moving very fast."

"Can't say I blame them. They make a beautiful couple. Is he a local lad? How did I not notice him before?" Sam ran her finger around the lip of her glass.

"You little minx! He's half your age and then some."

Minx? Now, where had I heard that word recently? Of course, Island Books. Robert the postie!

"Sam, do you know who would have the phone number for the postman, Robert Barrett. He lives on the mainland. I think he and Rachel were a couple. He needs to be informed of her death. It will be all over the island by morning. He can't find out on the ferry crossing on Monday morning."

"Unless he already knows." Sam replied cryptically. "Maybe he killed her in a jealous rage? Or as part of some perverted sex game. You said she was strangled."

"Nonsense! Really, do you think he could? Either way, I think I should call Inspector Lovington. It is possible that Robert was the last person to see Rachel alive!"

The 'Man in Black'

I t transpired that Inspector Lovington had taken a room above the Cat and Fiddle for the duration of the investigation. The function room at the back was to be turned over for use as an incident room. Sam had called PC Taylor to share our musings about Robert Barrett and he promised he would pass the information on.

PC Taylor was only a part-time constable and usually his presence and a few '*Watch out! Thieves operate in this area!*' signs were enough to keep a lid on budding crime waves in Wesberrey. His role until now had involved visiting the primary school to talk to the children about bicycle thefts and meeting local residents who wished to set up a neighbourhood watch scheme. He was obviously enjoying the opportunity of investigating an actual murder on his patch. True to his word, Inspector Lovington had called back to the Vicarage a few minutes later, and I agreed to pop down to the pub, sorry, incident room, after mass in the morning.

I awoke before sunrise with a heavy head from the wine the night before. *At least there were no more nightmares!* I was not much of a drinker, hardly even a casual one, and the two glasses I had had last night were making their presence known. Regardless, I had a service to prepare for and a sermon to finish. The Archdeacon would be presiding over the main event because I was still to be formally installed. This took away some of the pressure, but with all the drama of the day before, I found myself extremely ill-prepared for my first mass in my own parish. Wine or nerves or both combining, I soon found myself with my head over the toilet basin recycling the milk and cornflakes I had just had for breakfast.

"Are you alright in there, Aunt Jess?" I staggered out of the bathroom to be met by a very concerned niece, who was repeatedly stroking the head of the black fur-ball nestled in her arms like he was a fluffy stress ball. "I just came down to let Hugo out. He was scratching at my door."

"Yes, I'm fine, thanks. The milk must have been off. Are you joining me for mass later?"

"Of course, I wouldn't miss your big moment! By the way, Mum called last night to check up on things. I told her about poor Rachel Smith. She said she would get Grandma to call you later. Something about there being some history there with Rachel's mother?"

It was a shame I had missed a call from my nomadic sister. As Zuzu was older than me, she probably remembers a lot more about the Island's history than I do. I could have asked her why our mother used to drag us past the bookshop. Anyway, that would have to wait until later. I had a sermon to write.

***

The cold stone abbey was much fuller than I had anticipated. Almost three-quarters of the pews were taken with parishioners bundled up in their winter coats, hats, and scarves. Some had taken off their gloves to blow warm air on to their fingertips in a desperate attempt to warm them up. The mist from their hot breath made them appear like human dragons, their glowering eyes all urging me to get on with it and keep it quick.

"Thank you for coming to St. Bridget's on this frosty January morning. I really appreciate you all giving up your warm beds on a Sunday when you all would much rather be having a well-deserved lie-in with a soothing cup of warm coffee. I know I would!"

They laughed. Good start.

"Yesterday, we learnt about a violent attack on a servant of this church. In her own home. I am sure that many of you knew Rachel Smith, and all she did to serve this parish. It is hard for any of us to understand who would, or could, commit such an awful act against someone so loved within our community."

At this, there was a lot of murmuring and heads turning to their neighbours with hands covering their mouths.

"If anyone here knows anything that can help the police in their investigations, Inspector Lovington, from Stourchester Constabulary, is stationed at the Cat and Fiddle until further notice."

At the mention of the inspector's name, a new mumble washed across the congregation. I detected this wave to have a slight giggly quality.

I felt my voice rising. "A young woman has lost her life and a distraught mother has lost her only child. I am determined to help the police in whatever way I can. I urge you all to do the same. As a community, we need to work together at these difficult times and help each other as we come to terms with this tragic loss."

Regaining my composure, I returned to my prepared script. "Whilst the police search for Rachel's killer, we can take comfort in the sure and certain knowledge that she is being welcomed into her new heavenly home by our most loving father. Now let us pray. Psalm twenty-three, verses one to six: 'The Lord is my shepherd; I shall not want. He makes me lie down in green pastures. He leads me beside still waters. He restores my soul. He leads me in paths of righteousness for his name's sake. Even though I walk through the valley of the shadow of death, I will fear no evil, for you are with me; your rod and your staff, they comfort me...'"

***

"Fine sermon, Vicar, Nice and short, that's 'ow we like 'em. Psalm twenty-three, always a crowd pleaser. 'Ave to say it was a bigger crowd than usual. Must all be wantin' to see the new vicar," Phil shook me warmly by the hand. "Always 'elps to heat this place up, a good crowd. I put out as many heaters as I could without overloading the electrics. The old system just doesn't go near meetin' the climate requirements of those used to snug central heatin'. Early folk must've been made of sterner stuff!"

"You always do your best Phil, no one could ever accuse you of shirking. You keep this creaky old lady going and no mistake." I wasn't sure if Barbara was referring to the abbey or herself. Her eyes were fixed lovingly in Phil's direction until she turned to me.

"You are going to join us in the Vestry Hall for tea and a slice of cake, aren't you, Vicar? I see the Archdeacon has made a beeline for my lemon drizzle. Not the usual spread. I was a bit short-handed without Rachel on sandwiches." Barbara's voice trailed off as she tried to hold back the tears. "Who could have done such a terrible thing, Vicar? Really, I cannot get my head around it. Rachel caused no harm to anybody. She devoted her life to that shop, the church, and her invalid mother. If ever a woman was a saint, it was Rachel."

Phil put his arm around her shoulders and gently guided Barbara away to the hall.

"Invalid mother! She was a lush. Rachel will finally find some peace away from her." Rosemary emerged from the dark of the church alcove, muttering. "Vicar, I know it's your way, and I will defend our Lord's message to love one another until my last breath, but that woman... that woman. She killed her daughter years before someone pulled the scarf around her neck."

And with that, Rosemary disappeared into the vestry.

The church hall was heaving with parishioners, all wanting to shake my hand and con-gratulate me on a great sermon. I took that to mean nice and short so that they could escape to a much warmer room and partake of the impressive spread. Despite Barbara's protestations, she had excelled herself and there was ample choice for all. Three cake stands quaked under a load of red velvet and Victoria sponge cupcakes. There was a huge chocolate cake in the centre and around it stood an impressive selection of white chocolate and raspberry muffins and slices of lemon drizzle cake. There were no sandwiches, but I doubted anyone objected. It was a testimony to the void that Rachel left behind.

Tom and Ernest came in last, each carrying a pile of hymn books which they carefully put into the glass-fronted cupboards at the far end of the hall. Ernest walked over to me and handed me a couple of blue velvet bags weighed down with coins.

"A good offering today, Reverend Ward, lots of the higher value coins this week. Usually, we get a lot of copper. And quite a goodly amount of the paper variety as well. It would be wonderful to see this repeated next week, but I fear the novelty of a female vicar will probably wear off soon."

"That and a nice juicy murder. Word spreads here quickly, Vicar. Nothing like a scandal to drag the sinners in!" Tom said, checking out those who had assembled in the hall. "Don't recognise more than a dozen of the newcomers. I guess that is our mysterious 'man in black'. Now he looks familiar!"

Tom pointed to a tall man in a black trilby hat and long dark overcoat standing in the corner. He was standing next to a blonde lady with a large-brimmed black felt hat and a tailored red suede coat, its belt tied loosely at the back. I could not see her face, but even from the rear, she appeared to be a woman of style and substance.

"That's Arabella Stone! Lord Somerstone's heir. We never see her here. It would be wonderful if she were to start to grace our little congregation on a more regular basis. Her father has been a major benefactor to the wider community. Though he was not a churchgoer, he is a good man." said Ernest.

"It is really curious she should turn up here now. Perhaps she has a guilty conscience and feels the need to seek forgiveness in God's House?" whispered Tom.

"What would she be seeking forgiveness for?" I asked.

Tom readily accepted my challenge to dish the dirt. "Well, I am not one for gossip, but Rachel did mention once that Arabella Stone had turned up at their house one night. Oh, years ago. Rachel was still at school. Arabella was quite the celebrity back then, and, well, Rachel was really excited to meet her. But her mother sent her straight to her room. She told me she could hear her mother shouting at Arabella to 'Go away!' several times. Then the front door slammed and all she could hear after that was her mother crying." Tom mouthed the next sentence. "The visit was *never* mentioned again. But Violet, Rachel's mother, would get very angry whenever Arabella was in the paper. All very suspicious if you ask me."

Without even a pause to catch his breath, Tom threw his hands up to his mouth and continued. "Oh my, I've just had the most awful thought! You don't think it was a professional hit? Ernest, like in that mini-series we watched together on Netflix a few months ago. You know, the one where the mercenary was hiding out as a nun in a remote Mexican village and her orders were baked into a loaf of bread delivered by a boy on a mule."

"A contract killing?" Ernest scoffed.

"It's possible...." Tom pulled at the fingers of his tan leather gloves, shaking his hands loose as he talked. "But who amongst us could afford to hire a hitman?" he leaned in conspiratorially. "Lady Stone has the wherewithal, but what would be her motive? Maybe Rachel was her illegitimate daughter, that would explain the visit to her house all those years ago. Violet Smith was blackmailing her and now with Lord Somerstone on his deathbed, Arabella was worried that Rachel would claim her inheritance, taking a share away from her legitimate son and heir. So, she needed to get rid of her guilty secret once and for all!"

Ernest gave him an icy cold stare which immediately brought Tom to heel.

"Tom, that's a bit of a leap! For starters, how old would Arabella have been when Rachel was born?" I replied. "Watch out, she's coming over!"

"Reverend Ward! What a pleasure to meet you. I was just telling my friend Hugh how wonderful it is for the Church of England to accept women into the priesthood. A long time overdue if you ask me."

"Well, they have been letting us in for twenty-plus years now, so I think people are getting used to the idea." I smiled and shook her elegantly manicured hand. It was hard not to stare at her face. Once famed for her 'heroin chic' look, time and a hedonistic lifestyle had not been kind to her complexion. Her nose appeared to have been hollowed out, probably from excessive cocaine use. Even so, Arabella Stone remained a confident and, therefore, attractive woman.

"It's a great pleasure to see you here, Lady Somerstone-Wright. I hope you will become a regular visitor. High-profile members of the parish, like yourself, are always welcome. And your friends, of course. Will we have the honour of your son or husband joining us in the future, or perhaps your father, Lord Somerstone? It would be lovely to meet them."

"Yes, Gordon would love to come when he is next on the island, but he is away a lot in the city. I dare say you could use a wealthy benefactor. The church was perishing cold. I fear that school has beaten God out of Tristan, but he is good friends with the archbishop's nephew, they room together. As for Papa, if he hasn't made it through those oak doors in the last sixty or more years, I doubt we will be able to drag him in here now!" Arabella laughed and patted the man in black's chest in a very affectionate way. "Hugh, darling, could you see Papa sitting in that cold, damp abbey rubbing shoulders with the common people? Lord of the Manor he may be, but as he gave up his manorial rights long ago. I doubt he sees the need to act the part anymore."

And with that cryptic comment hanging in the air, Arabella laced her arm through her male partner's, and they made their way out the side door.

"Manorial rights? I asked.

"Ah yes, I imagine Ms Stone was making a joke about the ancient right of *jus primae noctis*. Or 'law of the first night'. Complete nonsense. There is absolutely no evidential proof that this occurred." Ernest answered in a very sombre tone. "Though Lord Somerstone had a reputation with the ladies, there was never any suggestion of impropriety."

"You would say that, you were his lawyer! No smoke without fire if you ask me," said Tom. "There were plenty of comings and goings at Bridewell Manor back in the day. And I can't believe none of you recognised the 'man in black'. Hugh? Hugh Burton, C'mon, the star of 'Above Stairs'. I despair! He was voted the sexiest man alive in both 1993 and '94! 'Rear of the year' in '91. There were rumours he was dating Arabella back in her 'It Girl' days, but his lordship objected because he was a fellow thespian. Strange to think he's allowed in the manor house now, but I suppose time mellows."

Ernest pulled Tom aside and was clearly remonstrating with him for his loose tongue. It seemed though that Tom wasn't the only person to recognise the famous actor.

"What a dish! Though he looks a lot older in the flesh and thinner. Well, they say the camera adds ten pounds. He was extremely polite and quite the gentleman about my cupcakes. Try one, Vicar. What do you think he's doing here, then?" Barbara led me to the trestle table. The same trestle table where Rachel had first shown me her plans for the morning room.

"I have no idea, Barbara. Just like I have no idea who would want to kill Rachel. I hardly knew her really, but I will not forget her. I hope it isn't too long until her killer is brought to justice."

"Well said Vicar, now... Victoria sponge or red velvet?"

The Postman Always Rings Twice

With Tom and Ernest looking after the Archdeacon, I travelled down to the Cat and Fiddle with Phil. Leaving him to check out the status of preparations for Sunday lunch in the pub's kitchen, I ventured into the back of the building where the function room was acting as a temporary incident room. The police had been most efficient, and the room was unrecognisable. In the centre were several tables acting as makeshift desks, with computer screens sat upon processing units with wires crisscrossing their way to electric socket extension cables. Also, on the desks sat black angle-poised lamps, buff-coloured notepads, and assorted pens. Around the edge of the room were large whiteboard stands on wheels which were already filling up with pictures of the crime scene, held in place by red and blue magnets.

Inspector Lovington was giving some instructions to PC Taylor, who was scribbling away furiously in his notebook.

"Ah, Reverend Ward, welcome to my office!" Inspector Lovington stood up and walked toward me. "That will be all for now, PC Taylor. Let me know when the other officers arrive on the ferry."

"Yes, Sir! Of course, Sir!" I thought PC Taylor was going to salute the Inspector, but instead, he just backed away into another room in the back.

"I suppose he's not used to investigating a murder. He seems very excited." I said.

The Inspector raised his left leg onto a chair and brushed his shoe with a handkerchief he had plucked from the breast pocket of his suit. A strand of brown hair dropped over his face. He swept it back into place as he stood up, carefully folding the handkerchief before restoring it to its rightful place.

"My apologies, Reverend Ward, but I seem to have gathered some green slime. Probably moss or something from the victim's house. Now, I understand you are concerned about the postman?"

"Well, yes, you see, I think he was having a relationship with Rachel. They didn't say as much, but I felt strongly that they were keen for me to leave the other day. At Island Books, Rachel seemed to be looking out for him and, well, he seemed disappointed when he found I was there. I think it killed the moment."

"Hmm, killed the moment... so you think the Postman was delivering more than letters on his rounds then?" He tilted his head and looked at me with a wry smile. I think the hardened police inspector imagined I would be embarrassed.

"With Rachel, yes. I believe he was expecting to get more than a cup of tea. Let's put it that way."

"Oh, so he was hoping for biscuits as well?"

I know he was trying to make me blush. "Inspector, I may be a priest, but I am a woman of the modern world, not a sheltered nun from medieval England. I can read the signs and Robert the postie was definitely expecting to empty his sack!"

The Inspector chuckled to himself as he pulled out the chair for me to sit down. "Reverend Ward, I apologise. Please sit down and I will take a full statement. Empty his sack indeed."

I explained to the Inspector all about my visit to Island Books, the wallpaper and Rachel's email. "So, you see, Inspector, Rachel was still alive Friday morning but was at home. I think she disturbed an opportunist thief who panicked and —"

"But how did she send the email?" the Inspector asked. "There was no laptop or computer in the house at Love Lane."

"But there must be... she told me she used to watch programmes online on her laptop as her mother didn't allow her to have a television."

The Inspector wrote a few words down in his notebook. "Unless she sent it from the computer at the bookstore, but you said she was off sick and didn't open that day."

"On Friday? Yes, she was sick. She emailed me at eight am to apologise and I know she didn't open the shop. The owner of Bits and Bobs didn't see her. His shop is next door."

"Reverend Ward, is it possible that Miss Smith lied about being unwell just to get out of decorating? You said yourself that she didn't agree to do it straight away. Perhaps she had other plans and didn't want to appear rude? Overnight, she reconsidered. Then went to the shop early to email you, before going home again." He looked up at me from beneath his brown lashes and smiled.

My breath quickened. Sam had warned me the Inspector came with a fruity warning label. "I really don't think so, Inspector. Rachel picked out the paper and paint. She had a mood board and everything. She'd ordered the paper even before I arrived. I can't imagine she would have let me down unless she was very ill. And if she was ill, why travel down to Market Square to email me, when I live only a hundred yards away from her house? Or she could have phoned, she must have the number for the Vicarage, she was an active member of the PCC."

"True. Well, I will enter all that information into the computer. I'll also ask my team to do a thorough search of the house for a laptop and see if we can trace the server for that message. Perhaps her murderer took the laptop. Maybe you are right, and it was just an opportunist thief, in which case the laptop will probably already be on eBay."

"Sam, I mean Dr Hawthorne, suggested that perhaps Rachel was blackmailing someone over a secret diary she had found in her shop. I don't think she was being serious, but that would also explain the missing laptop."

Ah, yes, Dr Hawthorne... Well, I will bear all this in mind. Thank you for your time, Reverend Ward. This is all very useful, and I will get my team right on it. If you think of anything else, anything at all, please call. This is my direct line." He handed me a business card.

"Inspector David Lovington, well Inspector, please do call me Jess. I really can't stand all this 'Reverend' stuff."

"Interesting. I actually quite like all this 'Inspector' stuff." With that, he took my hand and showed me back out into the pub lounge. I could have sworn I saw him wink.

***

I walked back up the hill to the Vicarage rather than taking the railway. *The exercise would do me good.* From the corner of Market Square and Harbour Parade, I strolled along the coastal path hugging Wesberrey Road as it gradually wraps itself around the Island, towards the old fishermen's huts. From there, the road steepens as it criss-crosses its way gently up the hill towards the junction at the bottom end of Back Lane.

I stopped and perched upon a rock perfectly placed to admire the bay beneath. Dark clouds cast their shadows upon the water and the handful of intrepid fishing boats that were returning home from their labours. The sun was sitting low in the afternoon sky and there was still a good half an hour's walking ahead before I would be safely back at the Vicarage. I needed the workout after all the cake I had been eating over the past few days. I had clearly forgotten, though, how long it took. Or more likely it was quicker when I was much, much younger.

I opened the Vicarage door just as the streetlights fired up, so I guessed it was around four o'clock. On the hall table, next to a squat green telephone, sits a retro answering machine, probably from the 1970s, that requires a cassette tape to record the messages. A red light blinks when a message is left. It was blinking. It made me wonder again why Rachel didn't call me to tell me she wasn't coming. That would be the quickest and most sure-fire way to ensure I got the message. Maybe she had, and I hadn't noticed? Maybe there is a message from her on the tape. A shiver went right through me. I wasn't happy with the prospect of listening to Rachel's voice now I knew she was dead. It took me several attempts to work out how to play the messages back.

They were all from my mother.

Bleep. "Jessamy? Jessamy? Are you there, Jess? Please, pick up the phone, sweetheart... Jessamy? Call me back, okay?"

Bleep. "Jessamy? Jessamy? Where are you? I have tried your mobile as well. Why don't you answer?"

Bleep. "Jessamy Ward. This is your mother! Stay away from Violet Smith and her daughter's mutilated remains.... Please, please just call me... I love you."

I didn't like the sound of the last message; it was rare for my mother to sound so scared. Mutilated remains! My sister, ever the drama queen, had obviously embellished the gory details. I called my mother straight back.

"Hi, Mum, sorry I had to go to the police incident room after mass. Then I walked back. It took me longer than I remembered. Are you ok?"

"Jessamy, I told you no good would come from going back there. What were you doing at that woman's house?"

"I was checking in on Rachel. She was supposed to help me with the decorating on Friday, but she was unwell, and as her shop was still closed on Saturday, I thought I would pop in. Just as well I did. Poor Mrs Smith was in a terrible state —"

"There is nothing poor about Violet Smith, toxic that woman, pure venom. Promise me you will stay away. Jessamy? Promise me."

"Mum, you know I can't promise you any such thing. I have a duty of care to all my parishioners, and she is a confused old lady who has just lost her daughter."

The phone went quiet on the other end. All I could hear was my mother's shallow breaths. Then gentle sobs broke through the silence.

"Mum? Mum, are you ok? Mum, are you crying?"

"I knew I should have told you before you went back there. I convinced myself that she couldn't hurt us anymore."

"Mum, you are not making any sense. Who couldn't hurt us?"

"Violet. Bloody. Smith, of course."

My mother's tone was suddenly more aggressive.

"Stay away from her! She's in the hospital, yes? Let them look after her. Please."

"But Mum, it's my job —"

"And I'm your mother. Honour thy mother and father, right? That's what you believe. Well, stay away, Jessamy, please stay away."

I promised to do my best to avoid Mrs Smith, but I wanted to know more. I wanted to understand why my mother hated this woman so much after all this time. It wasn't in my mother's nature to hold grudges. Whatever Violet Smith had done, it was obviously unforgivable in my mother's eyes. That did not mean that I should not forgive. I needed to find out more and decided that the best person to speak to would be my Aunt Cindy. I called her and arranged lunch the next day. Cindy only agreed when I promised to bring Freya with me. As Dominic would be there too, I didn't think she would take much persuading.

A Kiss on the Hand

Remarkably, for an island whose primary trade is tourism, there are only two places to eat during the week. The Cat and Fiddle serve the traditional English fare of steak and kidney pie, sausage and mash, roast beef, and Yorkshire puddings, all with the obligatory serving of garden peas. Alternatively, there is the Old School House, which as the name suggests, sits where the old schoolhouse sat before they built the new primary school in the 1980s. I checked out their menu on their website. Whilst the idea of a nostalgic trip back to my former school was very attractive, the eye-watering prices helped me decide to leave that treat for another day. So, the Cat and Fiddle won, and my choice had absolutely nothing to do with the possibility of seeing a certain police inspector whilst we were there.

"So, Aunt Cindy, why has my mother banned me from speaking to Violet Smith?" I asked when Freya and Dominic went up to the bar to order the food.

"Violet Smith? Darling one, why would you want to talk to her? I would do exactly what your mother says, my dear. Nothing good can come from talking to a woman like Violet Smith. Should we order some wine? I think we should get some water for the table. I'll be right back."

Cindy pushed her wooden chair back with such force it screeched across the wooden floor. Making dramatic apologetic gestures to the other guests in the restaurant, she joined my niece at the bar. I was now even more determined to find out what had happened between my family and Violet Smith to cause even my peace-loving hippy aunt to lose her cool. I was waiting to pick my moment to try again when 'you-know-who' emerged from the function room.

"Dave! Darling! I'd heard they put you in charge of solving this awful business. Come and join us! Have you eaten? Phil does a lovely lamb shank. Please sit. I understand you have met my niece."

"Ah, Cynthia, as beautiful as ever!" Inspector Lovington took my aunt's outstretched hand and kissed it. What is it with the men on this island? Is there something in the water? Or do all men behave like this around my Aunt Cindy? "Yes, I have had the pleasure of meeting Reverend Ward." This time I was sure I saw him wink unless he has a twitch in his eye. "But who is this?" He turned to Freya, who was obviously a quick study of these rules of gallantry and offered her hand just like a Jane Austen heroine. I was kicking myself for not doing the same.

Dominic stood up between Freya and the Inspector. "Inspector, may I introduce you to Freya, Reverend Ward's niece,"

"And you are?" The inspector sized up my niece's young suitor.

"Dominic, Dominic Creek. I am staying at Cindy's house. I'm an artist ... and a student."

"Wonderful. Well, enjoy your meal, lovely to meet you all. But I'm afraid I can't stay. There is a murder to solve." Dave smoothed down his moustache. "By the way, Reverend Ward, we traced the email you received back to the victim's house. It would seem you were right about there possibly being a laptop. If we can find that, perhaps we can find the killer. I bid you all good day."

"Oh, Inspector, just a quick question." I jumped out of my chair and followed him to the main door. "I was wondering if you had spoken to Robert Barrett. The postman? I hope you caught him before he set out on his round this morning. It must have been a terrible shock."

"Yes, I did. I waited for him on the first ferry. He was a little upset, but... well... he thinks you got the wrong end of the stick, Jess. He denied having any relationship with Miss Smith, other than delivering her letters and parcels. She sold a lot of books online and he would make her his last stop because she usually had orders for him to take away. He says he left shortly after you did on Thursday morning and, as there were no orders from the bookshop on Friday, didn't see Rachel again."

"Oh, I was sure there was a spark. I'm sorry to have wasted your time. By the way, Inspector Dave, if you don't mind me asking, how do you know my aunt?"

"Cynthia? She is an amazing lady. She helped me with... Well... It was nothing special, just... I'm sorry, this is really a conversation for another time." Inspector Dave looked rattled and slightly anxious. He was obviously uncomfortable. He made a point of looking at his watch. "Look, sorry, I really must be going. I can vouch for Phil's lamb shank. I expect I'll order the same this evening. Goodbye, Reverend Ward. Enjoy your food."

I walked back to the others. I was sure there was something going on between Robert and Rachel. Something didn't add up. That would have to wait, though. My lunch was getting cold on the table and my 'amazing' aunt needed to answer some questions.

Freya was already on the case. "So, Aunt, how do you know the dashing detective?"

"I did some work for him. It was a few years ago. It's not my place to say any more. Some things are best left to rest." Without missing a beat, Cindy turned to me, rested her chin on her left hand, and looked me straight in the eyes. "However, Jess, darling, I am dying to know what you make of our lovely Inspector. Like you, he is smart, intelligent, and single. He cuts quite a handsome figure, don't you think?"

Even though my heart was still skipping a few beats over that handsome figure, I wasn't in the mood to be distracted. "Aunt Cindy, please don't change the subject. My thoughts about Inspector Lovington are purely professional. Don't you try any misguided match-making either. I am not interested. And I'm certain the Inspector isn't either. So, Violet Smith. Tell me about my mother and Violet Smith."

"As I said, my darling girl, some things are best left to rest." Cindy started busying herself with her napkin. It was obvious she was hiding something.

"Aunt Cindy, I have a right to know. I can't work in this parish if there are secrets about my family I don't know about. It is my job to look after all my flock. I will visit Violet Smith this afternoon unless you can give me a jolly good reason not to."

I glared at my aunt and saw her normal air of confidence wither before me. Suddenly she looked every one of her seventy-plus years, her eyes watery, her mouth quivering. She took a deep breath and straightened herself up.

"Violet Smith killed your father!"

Let Sleeping Dogs Lie

"There. Are you satisfied now? I told you some things are best left to rest. You always were too inquisitive for your own good. Well, darling, there you go. That's why your mother took you away from here and that's why she doesn't want you helping that woman!" Cindy threw her napkin on her plate, stood up, regained her composure, did a quick turn on her heels, and walked straight out onto Market Square.

"Should I go after her?" Dominic asked, his eyes frantically searching for an explanation from me or Freya.

Freya bit her bottom lip, her whole body quivered. Bless her, she didn't know whether to cry or scream. She chose the latter. "You see! Grandma told you not to come back here. She warned you to stay away from Violet Smith. Oh my God! Did Mum know? See… Karma. A life for a life. Oh God, I can't believe that woman murdered my grandfather!"

"Freya, please. Cindy didn't say he was murdered. It might have been an accident." I went over to my niece and crouched down beside her. I took her hand and gave her a clean napkin to dry her tears. "This revelation is a shock for us all. Secrets are never a good thing. I understand you are upset. But all will be well. Dominic, why don't you take Freya for some fresh air? I will catch up with Cindy."

"Okay, erm… oh, er… it's raining?" Poor Dominic, his anxiety was paralysing. *Welcome to the family!*

"Okay, look, why don't you both stay here?" I opened my purse and pulled out some money. "Here, take this, have a few drinks on me and then make your way back up to the vicarage when it eases off. I'll see you back there later."

Where would my aunt go? She needed to clear her head, so a stroll along the front was likely, even in the rain. A few minutes later, I glimpsed her purple coat in the distance and sped up to reach her. The wind was picking up. I tried to call out, but the wind snatched the words out of my mouth and threw them out to sea.

"Aunt Cindy... please. Please wait! You can't say something like that and leave!"

Cindy turned to face me, her eyes swollen red with tears, the wind whisking up her long grey hair. "Some things are best left to rest." Cindy pulled me to her, laying her tear-soaked cheek against the side of my head. "How can I make you understand? Your father was a very handsome man. He was a good man. But he was a man. Men can be weak creatures."

Cindy stepped back and still holding my shoulders, nodded towards the covered seat on the promenade just ahead. We sat huddled together for warmth and support, looking out over the sea to the mainland. "Where to begin... you must remember they were different times. Society was experimenting with traditional boundaries. We were challenging the status quo. Darling, people were discovering the joy of sex. And your father? Well, let's say he was quite the explorer."

"You mean my father was unfaithful? He had an affair with Violet Smith?"

"Not just Violet. Darling child don't get me wrong. Your father adored your mother. He prized her above all others. She was his queen, of that there was never any doubt. That was why he married her." Cindy rummaged in her coat pocket for a handkerchief. "Your father is from one of the ancient families of Wesberrey. The Wards were second only to the Somerstones in power and prestige. They owned most of the harbour-front and the trade that took place there. The Somerstones had everything else that wasn't church land, barring a few outposts around the coast where the fishermen's huts were. He knew marrying a Bailey could mean no male heir. Michael didn't care. He married your mother anyway."

"So that's what Ernest meant by the shock of my father marrying a Bailey girl, but with all due respect, Aunt, that is nonsense."

My father was right, though. There was no male heir, just three daughters. My head was spinning. This sorry tale was crazy enough without bringing in a female witch line theory as well. I told myself that it was just a coincidence.

"I know you don't believe Jess, but Michael did. I do. Anyway, your father was a very attractive and sexually active young man. It was really only a matter of time before he hooked up with Violet Smith. Violet slept with anything that had a pulse. She had loose morals even by the standards of the day. You see, darling, Wesberrey attracted a lot of hippies in the late sixties and seventies. They loved the remoteness and the privacy it offered. Lord Somerstone would hold happenings at Bridewell Manor all the time. They say if you remember the sixties, you weren't there and there's a lot of truth to that. We thought we were living freely, but people got hurt. Love is never truly free."

I could feel my aunt crumpling as she spoke.

"Aunt Cindy, did you go to those 'happenings'?"

I could sense that my aunt had a deeper involvement in this story. Her breath was heavy, and she was being very careful about her choice of words.

"Of course, how could they not invite the village witch!" she laughed uncomfortably.

"And my Mum? And Aunt Pamela?"

"Pam? She was too square and Beverley, sorry your mother... no, it really wasn't her thing, but she accepted that your father went. He was part of that circle before they even courted. I only went a few times, and well before your father met your mother. As I said they were different times, and it wasn't all about sex. We experimented with art, music..."

Cindy stopped talking and looked straight out at the sea. Her chest seemed to rise and fall in time with the waves.

"Were drugs involved? LSD?"

"Yes."

"Aunt Cindy, how is this linked to my father's death?" I wasn't sure how much more of these revelations I could take.

"Well, Violet was a bit of a social climber. Her family owned the bookshop, but I doubt Violet read a single volume. She wasn't at all academic, but she knew how to use what nature had gifted her. And what it had given her was an incredible figure and wild black curls that reached down to the small of her back. She was an artist's dream. We were both so very young. At first, it was an adventure. It felt liberating. The idea of free food, free wine, and free love was intoxicating. Bridewell was always a party. There were film stars, musicians, and even politicians - all the rich and famous of the day. Violet and I had a lot of fun — in the beginning. Other girls came and went. It didn't suit everyone. I soon moved on to more meaningful relationships. But Violet stayed. She really embraced everything that Bridewell had to offer."

"And the men?"

"Free love? They really bought into the idea. It suited them. Let me rephrase that, it really suited men who already had an entitled sense of privilege. Men like Geoffrey, sorry Lord Somerstone, just expected to take whatever and whomever he wanted with no consequences. Men say there is a difference between making love and having sex. It suited them to think there were no strings; no payments due... and when you explain everything as art, well..."

Cindy was struggling to get the words out. She was choking on her own tears. I took her hands and turned more inward to face her. "Aunt, this is obviously too upsetting for you. It's okay if you can't tell me anymore. I understand."

"No, I'm okay, darling. It's just buried deep. It was a long time ago. Just give me a moment."

We sat in silence, just holding each other's hands.

Finally, Cindy took in a long breath and continued. "It had been ten years since the Summer of Love and hippies were a dying breed. Punk was in and times were hard. And none of us were getting any younger. Violet Smith wanted more. She felt she had paid her dues, and then some. She was drinking heavily. Violet would taunt your mother in the street, telling her about what they had done… What the three of them had done together, Violet, Michael, and Geoffrey. She wrote to Beverley. Nasty, hurtful, poisonous letters."

Recharged, Cindy hardly stopped to breathe. She talked as if her words were on fire and needed to be quenched by the sea air.

"I think it had dawned on her, Violet, that is, neither Geoffrey nor your father were going to leave their wives for her. She was nothing to them. Merely a… a plaything. Violet must've stopped taking the pill… anyway, she fell pregnant. I think she really thought that would change everything. It didn't."

"Rachel?"

"She was born about six months after Michael died."

"So, my father was —"

"Oh, darling, no! You only had to look at her. Rachel was definitely Geoffrey's child!"

"Lord Somerstone! So, Arabella and Rachel are sisters!"

"Yes."

This dreadful tale was making me feel even more compassion for Violet Smith, despite the fact she made my mother's life miserable. I had a lot of sympathy for this young woman - used and abused by the men in her life, including my father.

"This is awful, but I fail to see how Violet became the pariah here. She was the victim."

"Violet was a victim, but she wasn't an innocent. She was ambitious and scheming, and she had a vicious tongue. She knew what she wanted and was prepared to fight dirty to get it. The men took advantage, no doubt about that. But she was also playing a game. It was a game she was never going to win. She took a long time to see that but when she did…"

Cindy tensed her jaw and her fingernails dug deep into my hands. I worked my hands free from her grip.

"And my father? What happened to my father?"

"Violet wanted Michael to leave Beverley."

"But if she was still sleeping with Lord Somerstone and carrying his baby?" I was extremely confused. There was so much to take in and every word stabbed deep.

"There was no way she could have known who the father was back then. Not if she was still sleeping with both men. I think she really loved Michael. That's the tragedy - he is the last person she wanted to hurt. Michael and Geoffrey came as a pair. I'm sorry this is not an attractive picture of your father. Honestly, I think he just got caught up in the craziness of it all. But his behaviour, looking back, was inexcusable. Anyway, on the night your father died, Violet sent another one of her letters to your mother. She threatened Beverley and all three of you girls. Violet's letter described, in graphic detail, what she would do to you all if Michael didn't leave your mother immediately. Violet had crossed a line. Your father was so angry when he read the letter."

Cindy's breath quickened. She swallowed hard to pace her thoughts.

"Violet's family lived in Love Lane and your father went to her house to tell her to stop or he would go to the police. There was a terrible row. Violet's parents didn't know she was pregnant. It was such a shock to them. There was still a huge stigma around being a single mother. Especially to the older generation. Violet's father threw her out there and then. She ran after Michael, who was heading back toward the cliff railway and begged him not to leave her. I guess she was scared. Who wouldn't be? Maybe she slipped or tripped, or he slipped... but seconds later, your father was falling to his death from the cliff's edge."

"Mum said he died from a freak fall. So, it was an accident?" My mind raced around the recesses of my internal storage bank to recall all the times my mother spoke of my father's death, and I realised she rarely had. In fact, my mother had hardly talked about that day at all, or my father, except to tell us how much he loved us all.

"Maybe."

"Aunt Cindy, surely you don't think Violet pushed him?"

"Only she knows what really happened up there." Cindy replied. "Shortly after Rachel was born, Violet's parents took her back in. They both passed away a few years later. So, for all her dreams and schemes, Violet was stuck where she started, alone with a baby and that dreary bookshop. Your mother left. Violet couldn't."

I Don't Like Mondays

I took my aunt back to the Cat and Fiddle, but Dominic and Freya had already gone. The pub was offering a spiced gin and tonic special infused with cardamom, so I bought us both two tall glasses. We sat in silence, nursing our exotic drinks, unable to make eye contact. Cindy pushed around the ice with her slice of lime and sighed heavily. Her face was puffy from the wind, rain and tears and her normally immaculate straight grey hair was wild and knotted. I hated to think about what I looked like, but our appearance was the least of our problems. Cindy finally broke the silence.

"Darling child, you know your father loved you so very much, don't you?"

"Aunt Cindy, how did I not know something was wrong with their marriage? If my father was doing all that, how did I not know? Mum must have suffered so much."

"Jess, I understand it's hard to comprehend. Your father was like Jekyll and Hyde, I suppose. He led two different lives. He really adored your mother. She was on a pedestal. She was his queen. And part of a queen's role is to accept her husband's mistresses."

I was not sure I would ever think that this situation was okay, but it was forty years ago. If my mother accepted his behaviour, then who was I to question their relationship, even if it led to such a tragic outcome. It did explain why we packed up and moved away so quickly. I suppose it also explained why none of us returned to the Island for my father's funeral, nor for the casting of the ashes into the sea. My mother would have been very reluctant to come back here.

"So, did you go to my father's funeral?" I asked.

"Of course, he had quite the send-off. As I said, the Wards were a big deal around here. They sent their only son off in style. Your mother sold the house and never returned."

"And the rest of the estate? You mentioned the Wards owned most of the harbour front."

"After your father's death, his parents sold off their property. The Somerstones bought a fair bit. I believe your grandparents went to live in Portugal. They had a huge villa there, I understand. They cut all contact with you and your mother. I think they blamed Beverley for not keeping their son in check, but Michael was not a man who could be tamed."

It was true. I never saw my grandparents on my father's side ever again. I suppose I should have found that strange, but we were making a new life. I was thirteen and was more concerned with leaving my friends behind. My small family, my mother and sisters, were more than enough. We were happy and surrounded by love. I never felt that anything was missing — sadly, not even my father.

I left Cindy to walk back to her cottage on the edge of the harbour and made my way back up to Cliff View. It was eerie standing by the black railings at the top of the cliff's edge, knowing that this was where it all played out. I wondered if Violet Smith remembered what happened that night. I also wondered how she was doing. The Cottage Hospital was so close, I could see it from the path that leads up to the Vicarage. It would be so easy to take a slight detour and pay her a visit, but I had promised my mother, and I felt that, after all she had endured, I was duty bound to honour that promise. I loosened my scarf as I approached the front door and tried to turn my mind back to more mundane things.

I walked in to find Dominic 'comforting' Freya on the sofa in the lounge to the right of the hall. I scurried past.

"Could you take that upstairs, please? I am a vicar, remember? Behave yourselves!"

As I entered the kitchen at the end of the hall, I could hear muffled expletives and shocked giggling. Oh, what it is to be young, I thought as I reached up to grab the teapot from the wall cabinet. Then I had a brilliant idea. I had promised not to speak to Violet Smith, but no one had made my best friend forever, Dr Sam Hawthorne, promise anything! Making sure the hallway was clear of semi-naked young people, I rushed to the telephone. Fortunately, there was a handy list of '*important numbers*' taped to the table - the Cottage Hospital was at the top.

"Hello, Reverend Jess Ward here. Could I speak to Dr Hawthorne, please? Thank you. Yes, I'll wait... Sam, great, you are still there. I have a really big favour to ask."

***

"So... are you going to tell me why you wanted me to ask Violet Smith if she remembered your father? She did, by the way, Violet is usually a very vocal woman, but the mention of Michael Ward made her very morose."

Sam had come to the vicarage after work, carrying yet another alcoholic gift from a grateful patient, this time a twelve-year-old scotch whiskey. I told Sam all about the afternoon's revelation about my father and Violet Smith.

"Oh my! Never saw your father as a player. I mean, he was devastatingly handsome. I think the entire class had a crush on him, but still."

"I didn't."

"Of course not. He was your dad! Now that would be a very different story. Jess, I can understand your curiosity, but look how much this has upset you already. Do you really want to dig up more skeletons from the past? It was over forty years ago."

"Just tell me. Did she say anything?"

Sam refilled both of our cups. For some reason, I couldn't find the glasses. She made a play of making herself comfortable in her chair like she was about to tell a long fireside story.

"Well, as I said, she went very quiet. It was just like when we give a frenetic patient Lorazepam to calm them down. One second, they are kicking and biting you and the next they are curled up in a ball sucking their thumb. Anyway, Violet's reaction was as dramatic. I thought she was catatonic, but then she started to mumble. At first, it was hard to make out, but she kept repeating herself, over and over."

"And?"

The soothing taste of scotch was proving very efficacious as a tonic for steadying my nerves, but I was still in a state of anxious anticipation and Sam's milking of the tale was not helping. Did my father fall or was he pushed? Did Violet Smith murder my father?

"All she kept saying was - why did he jump? Why did he jump? Why? Why? Why?"

Lover's Leap

The dawn chorus found me already up and out. I had wandered down to the black railings at the cliff's edge and took time as the sun rose in the distance to say a quiet prayer for my father's and Rachel's souls.

"You're up with the larks this morning, Vicar,"

I turned to see Tom and Ernest shuffling towards me.

"Be careful there, Reverend Ward, the ledge is known to give way..." Ernest appeared to be quite agitated by my closeness to the edge.

"You know they used to call this spot 'Lovers' Leap'. It's said to be haunted by a couple of star-crossed lovers who jumped off the cliff hoping for an eternity together, rather than spend a lifetime apart." Tom said.

"Romantic nonsense, Reverend Ward." Ernest countered. "Don't listen to the old fool. People get all sorts of crazy ideas. At least we have the railings now. Health and safety is very important, People have been known to ... Oh my, oh I am sorry Reverend, what an insensitive oaf I am."

Ernest spun slightly on his feet.

Tom looked quizzically at him.

"Her father!" Ernest said in a full stage whisper, melodramatic hand covering mouth included.

"It's totally fine, Ernest, I promise. So, tell me, these railings weren't here then?"

"No, not at all. That would have been around '79 or '80? I think they installed these railings in the mid-Eighties. Built about the same time as the new primary school. A generous gift from Lord Somerstone, as I recall."

"So, Lord Somerstone paid for the school, very generous of him. Did his children go there?"

"Lord Somerstone only has the one child. His daughter Arabella. And she was at boarding school, of course. So, it was an extremely philanthropic gesture by his lordship," Ernest rubbed his gloved hands together and nudged his partner with a free elbow indicating it was time to move on.

A very generous gesture indeed. I wondered if it was one born from a guilty conscience, or maybe a way to provide for his secret daughter. I thought it was time I arranged to meet the lord of the manor. As his daughter Arabella had suggested, the church could do with a wealthy benefactor.

The Lord of the Manor

I found myself more than a little nervous about my appointment at Bridewell Manor. After all the revelations of the past few days, I was anxious about meeting the man who had possibly, indirectly, contributed to my father's death and the unhappiness of so many women. I was also speculating that perhaps Rachel's paternity had led to her murder. I could see no other reason anyone would want to kill her. At least I now knew that Tom's theory about Rachel being Arabella's love child was wrong, and the contract killing remained unlikely. Did Rachel discover that Lord Somerstone was her father? Was she blackmailing him, or Arabella? Or was she demanding her share of Arabella's inheritance? Or maybe she had confronted him - merely wanting to learn more about her father, and he wanted to avoid the scandal?

I also wanted to learn more about Geoffrey Somerstone's relationship with my father. From what my aunt had described, Lord Somerstone had been a very close friend, but quite a negative influence on him. So many questions. Naturally, I mentioned none of these issues when I asked for a meeting with his secretary. I had simply announced myself as the new vicar of St. Bridget's and explained that I wanted to introduce myself formally. Then made an appointment for the following day.

Bridewell Manor sits high above the rest of Wesberrey and dominates the island from almost every vantage point. There was a time when the abbey would easily have been the highest point but, as it now rests in a huddle of other municipal buildings on Cliff

View, its commanding position is diminished considerably. Bridewell Manor, in contrast, sits on a ridge overlooking the harbour in majestic isolation. Its 'Strawberry Hill Gothic' revival architecture, with white stone battlements and turrets, dominates the landscape. As children, I remember we imagined that princesses and dragons lived there, and maybe they did. It was hard to imagine my Aunt Cindy or Violet Smith being invited there as anything other than servants through the staff entrance. People like us rarely walked through the front door of such houses before the social revolution of the Sixties. Though I doubted they were ever truly viewed as equals. They were the guests of the Lord of the Manor and that, in itself, was arguably a sign of progress.

It is quite a bracing walk from the vicarage to the manor along the Upper Road. The Wesberrey Road coastal path runs all around the island and connects Harbour Parade with the other sea level locations. Then there are two main arteries that cross people and goods across Wesberrey. They are imaginatively named Upper and Lower Road. Lower Road runs from the back of Market Square in a zigzagging fashion linking the island's main residential areas. It follows ancient walkways that once provided farmers and fishermen with a route to market. Upper Road runs across the cliff top and old ridged pathways from Cliff View to the grassy leas on the other side of the island, cutting across its centre and linking all the municipal buildings and wealthier residential areas. The views from the Upper Road are breath-taking and, as there are no cars, makes for an extremely pleasant walk, whatever the weather.

I arrived close to the manor with about twenty minutes to spare before my appointment. I wanted to ensure that I had time to check my appearance, brush my hair and give my reddened complexion an opportunity to recover from my walk. There was a green-painted cast iron bench across the road provided for travellers to take in the vista below. The brass plaque screwed to the back slats instructed all visitors to '*Take a pew and enjoy the view*', which seemed an eminently sensible idea. The sun flashed off the clear sea, seagulls cawed from the cliffs beneath, and the wind had dropped to a gentle murmur. I sat down and allowed the natural rhythm of the island to subdue me. I tried to take stock of the drama of the past few days.

If I were being honest, taking stock is not the right term as that implies a clinical review of the presenting facts and I was way too emotionally invested in all of this to be that detached. I needed to gather my composure somehow, though, before I met with Lord Somerstone. If he was connected to Rachel's murder, I needed to keep that idea to myself. He could be a very dangerous man. Equally, I didn't want to get accusatory about his friendship with my father. The past was in the past and he was still the major landowner on the island. As the parish priest, I could not afford to go around upsetting prominent members of the community. I told myself that it would work best if I kept this meeting professional. There was plenty of time to find out more about his relationship with my father later.

Taking a deep breath, I walked up the final hundred yards to the gatehouse where the security guard checked off my name on his clipboard before pressing a green button on his desk that allowed me to pass through to the house. The gravel crunching under every nervous step slowed my walk up the driveway. Drawing closer, I could see that the large black doors of the house were open. Arabella Stone was walking down the path, extending her hand towards me.

"Reverend Ward! I saw your name down on Papa's diary. What a pleasant surprise. Did you walk from the Vicarage?"

"Why, yes... the views are exhilarating from this part of the island."

"Excellent! I am afraid Papa isn't as mobile these days and his man is still getting him ready for your visit. It takes an age to wash and dress him. Come with me, we can wait for him in the library. Have you had breakfast? Coffee, perhaps? I am sure Cook would oblige..."

Arabella led me through the impressive entrance hall. The white marble floor provided a contrasting backdrop to the blood-red carpet that poured down the central oak staircase ending in a circular pool at the base, the Somerstone gold crest floating at its centre. The family crest was echoed on the ceiling above, flanked by two enormous chandeliers, and everywhere I looked appeared to be covered in either mirrors or gold leaf. The decor was designed to take your breath away, and it worked.

"Terribly garish, isn't it? I always hated it. It was like growing up in Versailles. Takes an army of cleaners to keep it like this. When I am the lady of the manor, this is going to get a total make-under." said Arabella.

She guided me into the library.

"And all these books will have to go too. Talk about dust collectors, I doubt anyone has read a single one in the past hundred years!"

I looked around at the thousands of leather-bound volumes lining shelf upon shelf from floor to ceiling across three walls. The far wall featured a beautiful bay window and box seat looking out over an immaculate lawn leading off the side of the house, with far reaching views out to sea.

"This is a beautiful view," I said, moving towards the window seat to get a better view of the coastline in the distance. "What would you use this room for if not a library?"

"Oh, no idea. Haven't given it that much thought, to be honest. But no books. Maybe an indoor gym?"

At that moment, one of the offending bookcases opened up to reveal two men. One, who I took to be Lord Somerstone, an obviously frail old man in a wheelchair with his legs snuggly wrapped in a tartan blanket. The other was a tall thin man dressed in a black suit, starched white shirt with a cutaway collar and plain grey tie in a Windsor knot. As he was pushing the wheelchair and looked dressed for the part, I assumed he was a butler.

"Ah, Papa! This is the new vicar, Reverend Jessamy Ward. Reverend Ward, allow me to introduce you to my father Lord Geoffrey Somerstone, fifth Earl of Stourchester and Lord of Bridewell Manor." Arabella kissed her father on the cheek and took control of the wheelchair, dismissing the other man with a gentle wave of her hand.

"Did I hear your name correctly?" asked the old man, "Are you one of the Wesberrey Wards?"

"Indeed, I am. I think you knew my father, Michael Ward." I shook his hand and he gestured for me to take a seat at the mahogany table in the centre of the room.

"You are one of Michael's daughters? Really. Beverley Bailey's child? And a vicar? Well, I would never have seen that coming. Maybe there's hope for us all then." He laughed, then started coughing.

A cough that was just a tickle at first rapidly became a hacking torrent of concern for his daughter. Arabella knelt beside him with a white handkerchief, which he lovingly took to wipe his mouth. His rheumy eyes fixed on her in a pitiful way.

"What would I do without you, precious child?" he said as he rubbed her hand. "Please, could you leave us now? I want to speak to Michael's daughter alone."

Arabella nodded. "I will ask Cook to get us some tea," she said.

I thought I saw tears in her eyes as she walked past me back towards the entrance hall. It can't be easy to see a beloved parent in such a fragile state of health.

"Here, come closer so that I can see you better in the light," he said. "Michael's girl, eh? Which one are you? He had three, of course. Girls of your lineage always come in threes. May I enquire how is your Aunt Cynthia? Ah, sweet, sweet Cindy... I imagine she is still as beautiful as ever!"

I reluctantly moved my chair closer.

"Hmm, tilt your head to the light. Not unattractive. It wouldn't do to have an alluring vicar, I suppose." he coughed again. "I can see you take after your mother. Homely."

"Lord Somerstone!" It was all I could manage not to slap him across the face! Homely, indeed. Instead, I stood up and moved my chair as far to the other side of the table as possible.

"Sorry, didn't mean to offend you, my dear. There is nothing wrong with being unprepossessing. In your line of work, I imagine it's an absolute advantage! Some women are made to be wives and mothers, and vicars, and others..."

"And others? Women like my aunt, perhaps? And Violet Smith? What are they made for?"

"They were, probably still are, beautiful women. They're made to be muses. To have poetry written about them, to give to the world in a different way." Geoffrey Somerstone smiled. His eyes closed in joyful reminiscence of his former youth and his many beautiful muses.

"But Violet Smith is a mother. She was the mother of your other daughter. You must know that Rachel was yours." I leant across the table, hoping to see a reaction. There was none.

"Mine, Michael's, the milkman's. With Violet, it could have been anyone's." He answered, still lost in his memories. "She was very giving. So generous to us all. Man, could that girl party. Violet had a special gift. An unquenchable appetite for pleasure, in all its forms. But for your father, she would do anything. She loved him. I knew that. We all knew she loved Michael."

"But you still slept with her. Used her. You all used her. You made her pregnant and then abandoned her. My father included." I was struggling to stay calm and measured in my responses. I could feel the emotion building inside. Keeping this conversation professional was going to be a lot harder than I thought.

"Look, Reverend, I know what you are thinking. You see things in binary terms. Black and white. Good and evil. Right and wrong. The virtuous and the sinner. But I assure you, no one forced Violet to do anything. No one promised her anything, least of all your father. Make no mistake, Vicar. Violet loved to be loved. Lovemaking defined her. She revelled in her sexuality. Miss Smith was the raven-haired muse that called like a siren to the many artists that came here. She was a nymph. A Goddess. And she loved her role as mistress of the manor."

"And your wife? Arabella's mother? All this was happening in her house! And my mother! How could you?"

I found myself standing over the old man, raising my hand above his head as if I were about to strike him, crying hysterically. I had no memory of standing up or walking around the table. What was I doing?

I crumpled at his feet, sobbing.

Geoffrey Somerstone reached out his hand and gently patted my head.

"There, there, my child. Jess isn't it. Little Jess, your father had a nickname for you... now, what was it? Pudding, that was you, wasn't it? Your older sister Susannah was quite the beauty I recall... blonde, your father's eyes... she would have been about sixteen when he died. That would make you, what... eleven, twelve?"

"Thirteen."

"Really, thirteen, and your younger sister, Rosie? She was still at primary school. Terrible age to lose a parent. You probably don't remember your father that well."

I could not believe that I was sitting at his feet. It was such a child-like, submissive pose and yet I found I was unable to pull myself back up. As a priest, my role is to offer succour to the distressed and here was I unable to even stand. My stomach was a hollow shell.

"I asked your mother not to leave, you know." he continued, "I promised to look after you all. Your father was my best friend. I sent her cheques every month. She never cashed them."

"Guess she thought you had done enough." I doubt he caught the hostility in my feeble response. I pressed away my tears with the palms of my hands and looked up at the ailing old man. He was so thin and frail that it was impossible to believe him capable of causing so much pain. He looked at me with fatherly affection. It was as though he was oblivious to any concept that what he and my father had done was so morally repugnant to me. Or perhaps he knew but thought that his mores were genuinely acceptable, that all we shared was a minor difference of opinion. I got back on my feet and walked across to the bay window. I wanted, no, I needed, to see something beautiful.

"Did your wife know about Violet? Does Arabella know she has a sister?" I asked.

"My wife? Yes, she knew. At first, we all supposed the child was your father's, but as the years went by... it's a small place. The island. We would see the little girl in Market Square, down on the beach, everywhere. It was clear. Arabella, my darling girl, looks like her mother. Now there was a ravishing creature! It was the closest I've ever come to believing in your lot the day she agreed to marry me. Nothing short of a miracle, you see. But unfortunately, poor Rachel looked like me, except for her crazy black hair. There was no denying it. I offered to help. Violet refused. What else can a man do? No one wanted my money. I loved them all, you see, in my way. I would have loved Rachel, too. Pudding, please understand."

"Don't you dare call me that!" I swung around to face him. "And Arabella, does she know?"

"Yes, when her mother died, I told her. I thought, perhaps, that Violet would listen to Arabella. That she would let Rachel get to know her sister. Get to know me."

At that moment, as if she had been listening outside the door awaiting her cue, Arabella re-entered the room. "I went to the house on Love Lane one night to speak to Violet, for my father. But she wouldn't let me anywhere near Rachel. She shouted at me to 'Go away!' and slammed the door in my face." Arabella walked to the back of her father's wheelchair and kissed the top of his liver-spotted head. "Reverend Ward, may I call you Jess? I understand this all must be quite the shock. I have had years to come to terms with everything. Having a sister. My father's behaviour. I can't blame him. I was a party girl myself. Maybe it's in the DNA." She smiled awkwardly and rubbed his bone thin shoulders.

"Arabella, did Rachel find out? Was she blackmailing you?" I asked.

"Blackmail! Don't be ridiculous. I tried to tell her. I went to that awful shop of hers several times. All those dusty books. It's worse than this room, so dark. Anyway, I tried. Invited her to come up to the house, meet Papa. She was the very spit of him. But she called me a liar! She said her father was dead. An accident before she was born. Her mother had told her all about him. Rachel was convinced her father was Michael Ward."

"Rachel thought my dad was her father?"

"Yes, when she heard you were coming back to the island, she was excited to meet her sister. Oh, the irony! I suppose she was planning to tell you when you were alone. She said as much the last time I was in the shop. I tried to tell her, the silly girl, I showed her a picture of Papa with her mother I had found in a box. It leaves very little to the imagination."

Arabella went to a small wooden chest on the shelf behind her and pulled out a mono-chrome picture of her father and Violet Smith dressed in very loose togas with laurel wreaths in their hair. Violet was feeding Lord Somerstone from a bunch of grapes, her naked breast almost touching his open mouth.

"It's very... artistic," I said as I handed the photograph back.

I sat down on the window seat and stared out at the grounds. Rachel passed up a chance to be part of all this yet was excited to meet me. Was that what lay behind Rachel's plans to decorate the morning room? She wanted to get time alone with me. Just to get to know me when she refused to get to know her actual sister. Nothing made sense anymore.

There was a knock at the door and in walked the butler I had seen earlier carrying a tray of tea and biscuits, which he proceeded to lay out on the table before backing out of the room.

"You will stop and have some tea?" said Arabella.

"Of course, that would be delightful," I replied.

Everything Stops for Tea

It is likely that what happened next was the weirdest tea party since Alice fell down the rabbit hole. I half expected the Mad Hatter to yell 'next!' and all of us would move along to the next seat.

Arabella obviously had heard many stories about those halcyon or hedonistic days (depending on your point of view) and was prompting her father to tell us about all the times when. For example, they found Mick Jagger asleep under the grand piano in the conservatory. The puzzle not being why the lead singer of the Rolling Stones was unconscious under the musical instrument but more how it had got into the conservatory to begin with! Or the time when my father arranged for a pig race around the ballroom. Or the time when the two friends had challenged each other to a duel. It seems both parties swung at each other with broom handles from the two crystal chandeliers in the entrance hall until the loser dropped on to the pile of mattresses on the floor below.

"Well, at least someone was sensible enough to put down something to cushion your fall!" I said.

"That would have been Violet, I imagine." Lord Geoffrey replied, "No harm could ever come to her beloved Michael."

"So sad that she wanted her daughter to be Michael Ward's child so much that she refused to let us get to know her," said Arabella. "I so wanted to have a sister and now she is dead!

Who could have killed her, Reverend? It makes no sense. She owned a dreary little shop....
she was a nobody. But I..."

"You tried everything you could, my dear. We both did. Her mother wanted to make
believe she still had something of him left, I suppose. The question now is, what are we
going to do with her inheritance? I put money aside in trust for her. Just as I did for you
and your sisters."

"For me and my sisters?"

"Yes, all those unpaid cheques. I had my solicitor set up a trust for you all for when you
returned to the Island. Cindy assured me you would all come back one day. And here you
are! Well, one of you. You see, Michael was more than my friend. He was my brother."

"And your solicitor was?" I asked, but I knew already who it was going to be.

"Ernest Woodward, of course."

Of course.

***

I left Bridewell Manor with very mixed feelings. On the one hand, I was repulsed by the
alternative lifestyle my father, aunt, Geoffrey Somerstone and Violet Smith had engaged
in all those years ago. On the other, it was hard not to feel sorry for them all. Relationships,
no matter how casual, are never easy and I think, for all its unconventionality, there was lo
ve.

The other issue that was concerning me was how much of this story Ernest knew. As
Lord Somerstone's solicitor, he was instructed to set up trust funds for me, my sisters,
and Rachel. What aspects of this story was he privy to? I was confident that he would
protect his client's interests and that privilege would extend to the four of us, but who else
knew? And why hadn't Ernest said anything to me? Did my Aunt Cindy know, surely,

she would have mentioned it if she had? What about Violet? Did she know? Did Rachel? Did Rosemary?

I remembered Rosemary's whispered conversations after the first PCC meeting and after mass. She seemed to know a lot about Rachel's relationship with her mother. And she knew Rachel was strangled — with a scarf! This is a small community. I suppose she could have gotten that information from several people. Say, PC Taylor, or the ambulance crew who went to bring Violet to the hospital. Anyone else? And exactly how much money is in the trust fund? Is it enough to kill someone for? Who would benefit from Rachel's death? Would all the money revert to Geoffrey Somerstone, and ultimately Arabella?

As I approached the painted bench I had sat on earlier, I noticed that Arabella's guest, Hugh Burton, had taken my spot.

"Is your audience with his lordship over?" he asked.

"Yes. Why? Were you banished from the house whilst I was there?"

"Very astute of you, Vicar. I was strongly encouraged to take a morning promenade. Whatever you had to discuss with Arabella's father, they obviously didn't want any eavesdroppers. As you are done, I expect I can return to the warmth of the open fire in my room and a much-deserved hot toddy. I had forgotten how cold a British winter could be."

"Do you normally spend the winter abroad, then?"

"Yes, Arabella has a villa on the silver coast. I have rested there for the past few years."

"In Portugal? I believe my grandparents had a place there, too." I was sure that it was no coincidence that the Somerstones and the Wards both had homes in Portugal. It would not surprise me if they were neighbours. *I don't think anything will surprise me anymore.* "So, why are you back here this year?" I asked.

"Well, Vicar, just between you, me and this bench, his lordship's doctors have assured Arabella that her father's time is nigh. Enter centre stage - the doting daughter, bravely sacrificing her chance to catch some winter sun to be at her father's side. They said he wouldn't make it to Christmas and yet, he's still here. As a result, I have been lurking in the wings for the past three months, waiting for my line! I snuck over last week. Tristan, the dear fellow, arranged for the late-night ferry to surprise his mother. That poor boy will do anything to rile his father. Talk about a dysfunctional family! Boarding school is the best place for that kid. The further away from this place, the better."

"So, Lord Somerstone has no idea you are living there?"

"Not a scooby! He would go ballistic if he knew. He never liked me. That's no secret. He preferred her to marry that toad of a husband. Gordon invested in her title. It was a pure business transaction. But I get the bit that matters. He can never have her heart."

Hugh Burton stood up and walked to the edge of the path, the cliffs plunging deep below his feet and only the wide expanse of the sea before him. "Did you hear that Gordon, you toad? You will never have her heart. Do you hear me? Never!" His theatrical tones awoke the sleepy gulls beneath. As he turned to go, he stopped briefly to rub something off his shoe. "Bloody stuff. I thought I had cleaned it all off. Don't suppose you have any tissues on you, Vicar? Darn stuff left an awful mess on that hall carpet. I thought that butler bloke was going to kill me!"

The stuff Hugh was trying to brush off was a green slime, just like Inspector Lovington had on his shoe back in the incident room.

"Oh? When was that?"

"Not that it matters, but sometime last week... Wednesday or Thursday perhaps? Do you have a tissue or not?"

"Sorry, no. I had better be getting back to the Vicarage. Nice talking to you." I scurried down the path.

Did Hugh and Dave Lovington pick up the slime in the same place? The same place that I had seen it — Twenty-four Love Lane. If so, what was the A-list actor doing at Violet

Smith's house? I needed to call the Inspector and tell him about the moss. It might be an important clue. Or it might mean absolutely nothing. There's moss and green sludge everywhere on this island. The only reason I could think of for Mr Burton being at Love Lane was to do something for Arabella, but what would she need him to do? The original gossip surrounding the 'man in black' had been based on reports that this stranger had been seen sneaking around the island late at night. Perhaps Hugh had visited Love Lane one night during the week?

As I approached the junction, I spotted Robert Barrett's Royal Mail wrapped Piaggio Ape outside a house on the corner. I remembered he said that his rounds always started at the top of the Island and ended in Market Square, so I thought I could get a lift down. It would also be a good opportunity to find out a bit more about his relationship with Rachel.

I waved enthusiastically at a very uneasy postman whom I could swear was trying to pretend he hadn't heard or seen me as he wriggled back into his cab. "Morning Mr Barrett! A beautiful day, isn't it? Are you heading into town?"

With a dramatic shrug of his shoulders, Robert stuck his head out of the side window and grimaced. "Free island taxi service, that's me. I guess you want a ride!"

"Oh, thank you, thank you, so very kind. So sad about Rachel." I ventured as I stepped up into the van. "Who would do such a thing? Tragic to think that we may have been two of the last people to see her alive."

"Except for her mother. And the killer, of course!" he retorted, his neanderthal nostrils flaring.

"Of course, of course. Her poor mother. Why, do you think she could have seen Rachel's killer? How terrible! I wonder if the police have interviewed her yet?"

"No one would believe a word that old bat said. And that Inspector hasn't got a bloody clue. Seriously, that Sam Spade wannabe thought me and Rachel were having an affair, but I guess I have you to thank for that, don't I?" Robert glared at me, his nostrils and the vein in his forehead vying for first place in the 'who can explode first' competition.

"Mr Barrett, please be calm. Getting angry isn't good for your blood pressure. I only mentioned to the Inspector that you appeared close and that it wouldn't be nice to hear about her death whilst you were on your rounds."

"What do you know about my blood pressure? Rachel and I had a business agreement, that's all. I wasn't the only one, you know. The police need to look at that 'man in black'. And I am sure there were others. Like mother, like daughter. If you ask me, she probably deserved it. Who knows how many men she had on the go? Some women think they can treat men like their dogs. Well, I ain't no one's puppy!"

"Surely, no one deserves to die like that. You seem very upset about 'an agreement'."

"I think this is your stop, Vicar!" The brakes of the Ape screeched to a halt at the entrance to Market Square. Robert leaned across me to open the cabin door. "Oh, and Vicar, be careful."

Alarmed at this loosely disguised threat, I virtually fell out of the van and stumbled my way to the Cat and Fiddle. I told myself that having a menacing personality and a hatred of women does not make one a murderer, but I had a bad feeling about our postman. My suspicions weren't enough. I needed evidence to put him at the scene of the crime, and I didn't see any green slime on his shoes or in the cabin. Even if I had, that only proved he was on the Island, and I knew that already. Based on this level of evidence, the murderer could also be Inspector Lovington! The green slime was probably a red herring, but I still needed to share what I knew with the police and, to be honest, it was the only real clue I had.

The Cat and Fiddle

"So, let me double check I have everything down. Hugh Burton may have been at the victim's house because he had dragged green slime into Bridewell Manor on either Wednesday or Thursday night. Robert, the postman, had a 'business agreement' with Rachel Smith and said she 'probably deserved it'. Arabella Stone, the heiress, was the victim's real sister. Though Rachel Smith thought it was you. And both Rachel and your sisters are set to inherit a truckload of money."

Inspector Lovington had been diligently taking notes during our conversation and was now scratching his head as he read them back. His fingers lifted and separated his soft caramel locks in the most mesmerising way. Suddenly he stood up and closing his black book firmly shut marched over to the whiteboards where other details of the case were written up in various coloured markers. He bit the cap off a red pen and started to draw connecting lines between circled names.

"Well, I don't know how much is in trust for us, but yes... Erm, Dave, sorry, Inspector Lovington? Do you mind if I take a look?" I asked, edging my way closer to the boards.

"Actually Reverend, could you stay seated, please? Thank you... And you said that Rosemary Reynolds knew about the scarf?"

I reluctantly returned to my chair. The Inspector, meanwhile, went and opened the door at the rear of the room and called to PC Taylor.

"Yes, is that important?" I asked.

"Possibly. Ah, PC Taylor, you were the first on the scene after Reverend Ward. Is that right?

"Yes, sir. When I got the call from the Cottage Hospital, I was straight there. I was patrolling nearby."

"Did you tell anyone about what was used to strangle Miss Smith?"

"No, sir. Not a soul, sir." The constable shook his head so vigorously as he answered, I thought he was in danger of losing his helmet.

"And did the ambulance crew have access to the victim's bedroom when they collected Mrs Smith?"

"No, sir. I had taken all precautions to seal off the crime scene before they arrived. The door was closed and remained so until you went in."

"Thank you, PC Taylor. Can you escort Reverend Ward back to the Vicarage, please? Make sure that she gets home safely. Reverend, if you could just step outside for a few minutes, PC Taylor will be right with you."

"Inspector, I am perfectly capable of making my own way home. I don't want to take up valuable police time" I gathered my hat and gloves.

The Inspector moved over to me. Bending his head, he fixed me with his light brown eyes, which now bore a deeply serious expression. "Please, wait outside. I need to check a few more things with PC Taylor. Suddenly this motiveless burglary gone wrong appears to have a range of possible suspects with a growing list of motives. If Miss Smith's murder was premeditated, you could be in danger."

"In danger? From whom? Rosemary Reynolds? Don't be silly!"

Unfazed, he ushered me into the Lounge area and waved over to the bar. "Perhaps Phil could get you a drink whilst you wait." he suggested.

"Vicar, d'yah fancy another of our cardamom specials? On the 'ouse!"

I put on a reluctant smile for the benefit of my verger and walked quickly across the room. *Perhaps I could get some more local intelligence from the pub landlord.*

"Phil, that would be lovely. Tell me, how well did you know Rachel Smith? Over the past few days, I have heard so many different things, but I still can't see why anyone would want to kill her?"

Phil wore an unusually pensive look as he poured the warming gin cocktail into a tall glass. "Reverend, I guess we all 'ave secrets. Rachel was... what's the word? ... quite... enigmatic I s'ppose, in 'er way. She made the sandwiches for church every Sunday and for our meetings. She was usually very quiet. I used to joke she was our church mouse. I think it was just an excuse to get out of the 'ouse. That last meeting was the most animated I think I've ever seen her. She kept 'erself to 'erself. Not at all like her mother in her day, from what I've 'eard. It was Rosemary that brought 'er along to the meetings. I think she felt sorry for 'er."

"And why would Rosemary take so much interest in her?"

"Just bein' a good neighbour, I guess. Rosemary lives next door."

"Ah, I didn't realise they were neighbours. Has Rosemary lived there long?"

"Most of her life. She would've known the Smiths very well. She only went away for a few years after she got married. Very sad. Her 'usband died in an accident, lost at sea I 'eard. Terrible. Anyway, she returned 'ere. Took up a job as the school secretary in the new primary school. I think she used to walk Rachel to school when she was younger, and so on. Violet liked to drink. Often saw 'er in 'ere back in the day. Rachel was very different, but... everyone has their secrets."

After the revelations of the past few days, I had to agree.

Who's Wallpapered the Cat?

"**J**ust stay here, Vicar. I have strict instructions to check the Vicarage is secure," said an overly keen PC Taylor, enjoying his latest responsibility.

"Really, Constable, I admire your zeal, but I am sure I am perfectly safe in my own home."

"That's what Rachel Smith thought too, Vicar and look what became of her. Now please, allow me to do my job. Hmm, do you normally leave the door unlocked?"

I was just about to say, well yes actually, when PC Taylor pushed the front door hard against the hall wall and called out.

"Halt! Police! Who goes there?"

There was the sound of crashing wood and metal from inside, and a streak of squealing black fur ran out under my legs.

"Hugo!"

A copper-topped banshee wearing a blue gingham headscarf followed, pushing a startled PC Taylor against the open door as she passed.

"Freya!"

I called after my niece and helped her gather up the terrified cat. With her arms full of black fur, Freya confidently strode back past PC Taylor, puffing up the loose ginger curls that had escaped their checkered prison.

"Pfft, what on earth were you doing? You scared the poor thing half to death! There, there Hugo. Did the nasty policeman scare you? Paste and paper flew everywhere! God knows what you were thinking." In a much softer tone, she called out, "Dom? Are you ok?"

A very muffled "yes" answered.

A crest-fallen PC Taylor and I walked into the morning room to see a mass of brown curls wriggling free from underneath a blanket of wisteria. Dominic and Freya had obviously been busy. Most of the paintwork had been done, and they were about half-way through the papering. Aside from the gloopy mess on the floor, and the wooden stepladder now perched precariously against the trestle table, the room looked much better. Rachel's taste in wallpaper was an inspired choice.

I rushed to help the young man up onto his feet.

"No need to fuss, I am fine... ouch!"

"That doesn't sound fine to me. We had better take you to the hospital. PC Taylor, could you give Dominic a strong arm to lean on? I know it's only a few hundred yards away, but he might have broken something."

"Please, Reverend, I am okay, honest. Urgh, what a mess! Freya and I wanted to surprise you. We thought it would be a nice way to... Aaaw, that smarts!" Dominic leant on the trestle table with one hand, holding his head with the other.

"I really think we should get you looked over just to be sure. PC Taylor?"

"Yes, Reverend. Come here, lad. We will soon get you sorted out. No need to bother yourself, Reverend. Miss. I've got this. Feel like I am somewhat to blame." PC Taylor cast a sheepish eye at Freya, who nodded firmly in agreement.

"Thank you, Constable, you were only doing your job. I appreciate it. And Freya, apologise to the officer."

Freya, still holding the lava-eyed black bundle that had probably contributed most to the current predicament, gently stomped her foot and with a petulant shake of her shoulders reluctantly apologised.

"Ok, good. Well Constable, if you could take care of Dominic, my niece and I will clean this up."

With Dominic and PC Taylor gone, I wanted to talk to Freya about everything that had been going on. I hadn't had the chance to discuss with her what I had found out about Violet Smith and her grandfather, and to be honest, I wasn't looking forward to sharing what I had learnt.

"Please, Freya, put the cat down." I said as I struggled to lift the fallen stepladder. "We need to talk."

"If we must. I am suddenly very tired. Let's go into the kitchen. Hugo needs something to eat."

Freya drifted into the kitchen and absent-mindedly pulled out a tin of cat food from the cupboard. Hugo stretched his front legs over her bent arm and onto the worktop, his curled tail flicking her face. I followed behind in my own trance-like state. Recent events had taken their toll on us both and this last burst of drama had sapped both our energy stores.

"Tea?"

"Yes, lovely, thanks. Freya, I need to talk to you about your grandfather."

She sighed. "Talk away!" Freya purposefully busied herself with the kettle and tea things.

"Your grandfather and Rachel's mother had... hmmm, let's describe it as an unconventional relationship. She was a very troubled woman, and well, she brought up Rachel to believe that your grandfather was her father. He wasn't, but he could have been."

"I know. Aunt Cindy explained everything when she was here earlier. She helped with the skirting board. For a woman of her age, she is incredibly nimble. She had no trouble at all kneeling down all that time. I was exhausted just watching her from my position holding the stepladder."

"All those years of yoga, I guess. Did she tell you who Rachel's father really was?"

"Yes, Lord Somebody or other. The family with the big tomb in the graveyard."

"Did she say anything else?"

"Not really, just that she was so sorry about Rachel and that she should have seen it coming. But she had a bit of a red mist where Violet Smith was concerned."

Freya slid my freshly made tea across the table and sat down opposite me. Something was obviously bothering her.

"How could she have expected to see it coming? She's not psychic!"

"Isn't she?"

"Of course not." I laughed.

Freya leaned across the kitchen table, nursing her teacup with both hands. "How are you so certain?" Her cornflower eyes searched mine for answers.

"Because... because there is no such thing! Cindy shouldn't be filling your head with this witch nonsense. She is no more psychic than I am!"

Freya drew her cup to her lips and stopped short, choosing to swirl its contents around instead. "Tea is a fascinating drink, isn't it? It's just a hot water leaf infusion, but unlike chamomile or peppermint, which both make excellent drinks, in their own right, tea, real tea, breakfast tea, is much, much more than a warm drink. It is magical. Transformative. Restorative. A ritual. A bonding agent. A reason to stop, to contemplate, to meditate." She mused.

"Yes, I suppose so... what has this to do with Cindy's psychic pretensions?"

"Well, the way I see it, and maybe my anthropological studies have taught me this but, the way I see it. Humans need magic. We need ritual. We need belief. We need God and goddesses and tea. What makes your beliefs truer than Cindy's or better than this cup of tea? They can all restore the soul."

"You are comparing my love of God with a cup of tea?" The very suggestion was shocking to me.

"Well, right now this cup of tea is offering me more comfort than your God, so yes, I am. Please, Aunt Jess, I am not challenging your faith just asking you to be open to accepting others. Cindy believes that you and I will carry on her traditions. Perhaps she is right. Perhaps her world is no more magical than this cup of tea. I want to learn more and to learn we must first allow our world views to be challenged."

So that's what was bothering my young niece. Who knows what Cindy had been filling her head with all day? I would need to have another chat with my elderly aunt, but for the moment, I would let it pass. We continued to drink our tea in silence. Then, whether from an uncomfortable need to move on the conversation or a sudden recollection that a certain young man was lying on a nearby hospital bed (probably both) Freya suddenly jumped out of her chair.

"Anyway, I really think I should go to the hospital to check on Dom. I will take some cat food up to the graveyard on my way." Freya threw the remains of her magical cuppa into the Belfast sink and grabbed her coat and hat from the rack near the back door.

"Thanks. See you in the morning," I said, grateful for the change of subject. "I have to prepare for the parish sub-meeting tonight. All this drama has meant that I have seriously neglected my parish duties. It's going to be a long night for me." I walked to the door and kissed my niece on the cheek. "We can discuss more of our crazy family history some other time. I am sure Dominic is okay. Off you go, and try not to make too much noise when you come in."

"Oh, before I forget, we found a book in with the wallpaper. Let me just get it for you."

Freya returned with a slightly battered copy of Julian of Norwich's 'Revelations of Divine Love'. She was reading the back cover. "What's an anchoress?" she asked.

"A medieval nun who cut herself off from society for a strict life of religious contemplation. They were usually bricked up next to the parish church, and they provided advice to visitors whom they spoke to through a small window in the side of their cells."

"Sounds fun. Well, it says here that she wrote this book after having a series of visions. I guess if she wasn't a nun, they would have called her a witch? Just like our ancestors. How is she any different to Aunt Cindy, eh? Anyway, I must go. I will leave this with you. Looks interesting."

***

As I settled at my desk to work through the fresh pile of papers marked for my attention, I wrote '*tea analogy*' and '*divine love*' in my sermon ideas notepad and pondered on Freya's observations. She was right about at least one thing. There is magic in ritual and one of my most effective rituals was mind-mapping ideas for sermons. Perhaps, I thought, it would also help me work out who killed Rachel?

I turned to a clean page and wrote Rachel's name in the centre and circled it, several times. Then I drew spokes radiating from the centre and added the names of the suspects. From not having a clue who would want to kill Rachel less than a week before I now had quite the list. Hugh Burton, Arabella Stone, Lord Somerstone (though I thought it unlikely to be him, given his frailty - unless he got his butler to do it?), Rosemary Reynolds (as I still did not know how she knew about the scarf) and Robert the Postie. I supposed that Violet could have killed her daughter, but this seemed unlikely, and again, her frailty probably ruled her out. Was there anybody else? And what about motive? Opportunity? Perhaps the answers were in the leaves of that magic tea Freya had made. If only I knew how to read them. I guess my aunt would know how.

I shook myself. *What crazy nonsense!* My head thumped. It had been an emotionally exhausting day. It was unbelievable how close I came to hitting Geoffrey Somerstone earlier, and then I was crying at his feet! I didn't recognise myself in such erratic behaviour - acting like an angry teenager. Such an uncontrolled emotional response was terrifying. I was always the rational one. The calm one. And now all this talk of magic tea and witches...

I needed guidance from Him upstairs, so I sat back in my chair and took advantage of an empty house to take a quiet moment to pray. My family may struggle to understand, but my faith centres me. Prayer always helps me to anchor in a safe harbour when the seas of life are stormy. I reminded myself that my reaction was a natural response to a stressful and confusing situation. I was feeling seasick, that was all. With God's strength, I would work through this. Right now, I needed to get back to the task at hand. I took a deep, fortifying breath.

On the top of my 'Urgent' pile was an official letter from the diocesan secretary confirming plans for the Bishop's visit for my collation, installation and induction on the 1st February. The feast of St. Bridget. It was now less than two weeks away. Well, there was my lighthouse, and with faith, I would safely navigate the rocks ahead.

A Crisis of Faith

As I braved the short walk to the vestry, the frosty evening air jabbed its icy fingers into every bone of my body. This time last week I had felt the excited, if anxious, glow of chairing my first PCC meeting. The same meeting at which Rachel had shared her plans for the morning room. Last week I had stood outside the vestry door planning to make a grand entrance. Now I stood outside the same door, wishing I could turn around and slink quietly back home. Except I didn't really have a home, did I? This time last week I was rejoicing in the thought of finally having a place where I and my glass fish collection could settle down and now, I wasn't so sure that I would ever feel settled here.

My installation was still two weeks away. I could withdraw. Return to the mainland, talk to the Archdeacon, explain my reasons to the bishop. I felt so tired. They would understand. Everyone would understand. This was, after all, not the most auspicious start to my ministry. I had opened Pandora's box by coming back here. Maybe my mother was right, and it would be best all round if I left. My emotions were see-sawing. One minute I had faith in God's plan bringing me here and the next...

I placed my hand firmly on the black iron handle, as I had done only a week before. This time I anticipated its stiffness, and, with significantly more grace, I entered the room. There was no trestle table this time. Then I realised there wouldn't be, that was back in the morning room. There was only Phil, Barbara, Tom, and Ernest huddled together in a circle of chairs around an old electric fire. No Rosemary. No other members of the PCC. And, of course, no Rachel.

"C'mon Vicar, pull up a chair. It's cold enough out there to freeze the Devil's 'orns off!"

"Blimey Phil, what a thought! You are a card! Vicar, there's a flask of warming tomato soup in my bag here for you when you are ready. I doubt you have had much to eat with everything going on. I'll pop the kettle on. There's a tin of walnut cake in the kitchen. I'll bring it through."

Barbara and Phil were their usual bubbly selves, casting flirtatious hooks into the conversation for the other one to catch. Tom and Ernest remained wrapped in their matching grey winter scarves and coats for the whole evening and looked even more like their muppet doppelgangers than last week. Each person proved to have a tight grip on the events calendar for the coming week, and they all seemed genuinely pleased to be working with me. We had a productive meeting, talking through the flower arrangements and catering plans for my installation, as well as the day-to-day management issues of the church. The soup and cake were delicious. I found the homemade food and wholesome company helped to settle my soul. I was growing exceedingly fond of my little team. If they were still prepared to have me as their shepherd, then I would find a way to stay. I was blessed indeed — they were good people.

The Importance of being Ernest

I was determined to get a private word with Ernest before he left. I needed to find out what he knew about the trust funds and Rachel's paternity.

"Reverend Ward, with all due respect, I really do not think this is the time or place to discuss pecuniary matters."

"With all due respect Mr Woodward, I think this the perfect time. Who else knew about Rachel's trust fund? Would it amount to a significant enough sum to murder her over?"

"I cannot speak to what sum of money would ever be enough to kill someone for. But, to my knowledge, the only people privy to the trust's existence were his lordship, Lady Arabella, and myself. And I can assure you, I do not benefit from the death of Miss Smith!" Ernest stood resolute. His voice remained measured despite the obvious pique that was growing inside him at the merest suggestion of any impropriety on his part.

"I am not suggesting you would benefit or acted inappropriately in any way. Ernest, do you think Arabella could have seen Rachel as a threat to her inheritance? She says that she tried to tell Rachel the truth, but what if she was scared that my coming to the Island would bring everything out in the open? That once the truth was out, Rachel would demand what was rightfully hers. Perhaps even more than her trust fund, say, an equal share of the estate? Now that might be worth killing over." The thoughts I was verbalising shocked me. There was a possibility that my return to the island could have been a catalyst for this tragic event.

"Reverend Ward, I suggest if you have any evidence to back up these wild accusations, you inform the police straight away. Otherwise, may I remind you that without such evidence, you are in danger of committing slander." Ernest waved across the room to Tom, indicating that our conversation was over.

"Ernest, I'm sorry. Just one more question, please. The trust fund for me and my sisters. Why did you not tell me about it when I arrived?"

"Because, Reverend Ward, there is a caveat. Until the death of his lordship and the return of all your siblings to live on Wesberrey, no one can access the fund. His lordship is very much alive, and your sisters are residing elsewhere. To have told you might have influenced your decision to take up the position of parish priest at St. Bridget's. I needed to be certain you were choosing to be here for the right reasons. Now, if you will excuse me, Tom has a lamb stew approaching perfection in the slow cooker, and the latest episode of Midsomer Murders starts in ten minutes."

"Of course, please give Tom my apologies for holding you up. And Ernest, thank you for your candour."

He smiled. "Just doing my duty, Reverend Ward. Have a good evening." Pressing his gloved hands together, Ernest Woodward bowed his head and walked off briskly to join his partner. I was slightly envious of their relationship, and that stew sounded wonderful.

The Fog comes on Little Cat Feet

The freezing night had morphed into a foggy morning. Earth-trapped clouds wrapped themselves around the gravestones as I set off towards Love Lane. Freya had snuck in without a sound during the night and was late to breakfast, but I knew from her text that the hospital was keeping Dominic in for observation in case of concussion. I had several parishioners to visit that day, but first I wanted to pop in to see Rosemary. I had not expected to see her last night. As treasurer, she does not attend the operational PCC sub-meetings. I wanted to find out more about her relationship with Rachel and how she knew about the scarf.

I could make out the silhouettes of Hugo's feral friends weaving between the carved marble stones or sitting imperiously on top of them. They appeared to move as one with the fog, which reminded me of a poem I had once read. I tried to recall the words and author as I cut through to Rosemary's house. Was it Carl Sandburg or Walt Whitman?

"So lovely of you to call in, Vicar. Reverend Weeks was a frequent visitor before his illness." Rosemary brought in a white plastic wicker tray with red handles, laden with an ornate gold-edged floral china tea set. Digestive biscuits stacked precariously high on the centre plate. "He loved to catch up on all the island gossip over a cup of tea. We had a shared interest in horticulture. His herbaceous borders were a year-long mission. He always maintained that the winter could hold as much majesty as the summer's gaudy hues."

Stuffing a biscuit into my mouth between gulps of tea, I nodded in agreement. "The garden looks wonderful," I said when I finally emptied my mouth. "As does your garden at the front of the house. Such a contrast to the Smiths next door. I imagine it is frustrating to have your beautiful climbing roses and clematis under attack from the bindweed."

"I used to help Violet with the garden and the house when Rachel was small. She had so much to cope with, being a single mother, the shop and everything. Violet was not very domestic. I babysat Rachel several nights a week to let her mother go out. Often, Violet would come home steaming drunk and I would stay with Rachel, just to be safe, you know. Eventually, it was easier to make up a bed for Rachel here to get her ready for school in the morning and so on. I worked in the school, you know, so it was no trouble to take her in with me."

"I am sure Violet appreciated your support."

"Violet! Appreciate my support! Vicar, you obviously do not know Violet Smith. She called me an interfering old busy-body. Called me a lot worse when she was drunk. But she still took my help, especially if it meant she could go out, meet up with her fancy men and get pickled! Then, as soon as Rachel was old enough to get herself to school, Violet cut me off dead. That poor child had to do everything. I helped when I could. Tidied up the garden when they were out. Sometimes I slipped in to check there was food in the cupboards and did a bit of cleaning up."

Rosemary held a digestive in mid-air, lifting it up and down as she spoke, but never took a bite.

"So, you had a key to Violet's house?" I asked.

"Of course. How else would I have got in and out? The problem was, as Violet grew older and the men stopped buying her drinks, she stayed in more and became a recluse. I don't know what is worse, a promiscuous drunk or a lonely, bitter one. Rachel left school, took over the shop, and... I tried to help. I really did, Vicar." Rosemary put the biscuit back on the plate in front of her and paused. "I invited her to join me for Sunday lunch, tidied the garden. At first, she seemed grateful, but later Rachel spurned all my suggestions. All except one, when I invited her to join me going to church."

"That is interesting. Why do you think she wanted to go with you to church?" Rachel was a member of St. Bridget's PCC years before there was any suggestion that I would take over as the parish priest. There must have been another motive.

"At first it was just to get out of the house, I think. Perhaps walking with me on a Sunday morning reminded her of all those mornings we walked to the school together..." Rosemary's eyes grew tearful. "She only wanted to be loved - the poor girl. Imagine living with that woman. Listening to her poisonous view of the world every day. Never being able to do enough. Be enough. Some women do not deserve the gift of a child. I think, sometimes, God makes terrible mistakes. Maybe he is more human than we are."

"God does not make mistakes Rosemary, but his ways are not always easy for us to understand," I said, only half believing what I was saying myself.

It did sound as if Rachel had had a terrible life and it would explain why she so desperately wanted to engage with me if she believed I was family. A parent's words hold so much power. Violet's obsession with my father had denied Rachel the gift of getting to know hers.

"Rosemary, did Rachel talk to you about my father at all?"

"She rarely spoke of anything else! I tried to warn you, Vicar. I knew Michael Ward wasn't her father. Can't forgive Violet for lying to her own daughter like that. The more I tried to tell Rachel the truth, the more she accused me of interfering. Our last conversation, on the road back from the PCC meeting, she was so excited about helping you with the decorating. All that talk of finally getting to know her sister. What great friends you would become. Such a fantasy! I had to put her straight. I had to. But she wouldn't listen. She called me terrible names. Said such hurtful things. So did I. Vicar, I am so very sorry. My last conversation with her, if I had known, I wouldn't have said so much. The last words I said to her were..." Rosemary broke down and mumbled the rest into a paper napkin, "I called her... an ungrateful cow. Like mother, like daughter. And I wished she was dead!"

My hands reached out to take her trembling ones to comfort. I could feel Rosemary's shame and grief through her thin, pearlescent skin. It was consuming every part of her. I knew Rosemary was not Rachel's murderer. She had loved her as her own daughter. What I still did not know was how she knew about the scarf.

"Rosemary, you were angry and upset. It is obvious you loved Rachel very much. I am sure that she knew that, deep inside. Her death must be very hard on you, but you cannot blame yourself. Perhaps you can help the police find her killer. Maybe you know something that will help, as you knew her so well."

"I can do better than that, Vicar. Wait here..." Rosemary slowly eased herself out of her chair and moved towards the oak sideboard on the other side of the sitting room, where she opened a drawer stuffed full of papers. Reaching underneath them, she pulled out a small laptop. "I know it was wrong to take this, but... I saw you run out of the house on Saturday morning. No offence, Vicar, but you don't look like the type to exercise much, so I knew something was wrong. I thought it must be Violet. That the devil had finally claimed his own. But when I went upstairs, she was screaming large as life. Then I found Rachel, my poor sweet child. I guessed you had found her too and were on your way to get the police. I couldn't let anyone find this. Rachel had confided in me once about her 'on-the-line' business and that she used this contraption. There's supposed to be a camera in it somewhere." Rosemary turned the laptop upside and down trying to figure it out. "She was more like her mother than I wanted people to know."

The Way to a Man's Heart

I waited with Rosemary until Inspector Lovington and PC Taylor arrived to interview her and take the laptop into evidence. I had a busy day of appointments ahead, so made my excuses and left as soon as possible. However, I stayed long enough to learn that Rosemary was concerned that people would find out about Rachel's online activities and that the laptop had been open on the dressing table facing the bed when she found it.

It was intriguing, and I will admit being very tempted to stay with the inspector a while longer (the navy double-breasted designer suit he was wearing fit him extremely well) but he had his job to do, and I had mine. Not only that, but the police inspector's body language had made it as clear as a Swarovski crystal that he was not at all happy with Rosemary withholding vital evidence in a murder inquiry. He wanted to get on with the interview and move on swiftly with the investigation. There was no time for idle gossip with the local clergy.

As the sun fell behind Cliff View, I made my final trek of the day up to my front door. Hugo sat patiently on the mat and curled affectionately around my legs as I pushed it open. Maybe I should start locking the door, I thought as I called out towards the delicious smells drifting from the kitchen.

"Freya! Is that you cooking? Smells wonderful."

Freya emerged from the end of the hall, wiping her hands clean on a green tea towel.

"I hope you don't mind, but I wanted to cook Dom something nice. He says that the hospital food is hideous. I also invited Dr Sam over to join us, didn't want you to feel like a gooseberry all evening."

"Very thoughtful. Can't have your old spinster aunt ruining the romantic vibe. What time are we eating? I'm famished."

"Well, the recipe on the internet said it takes two hours. So, I am a little ahead of myself, but I still need to cook everything else. Haven't even started on the dessert yet. Need a shower... I was planning to just warm it through. Or will that old host trolley keep it warm? Anyway, I told Dom and Sam to be here for eight."

"Eight! That's hours away. I might just grab a quick snack to tide me over. Is the hot water on, then? Did you want to go first? I really need to eat."

I walked into the kitchen to discover the remains of a chimp's tea party. Well, what would have been the remains if they had been trying to make beef bourguignon. It was cute to watch my care-free niece trying so hard to impress Dominic. *It must be love.*

As Freya hadn't followed me into the kitchen, I guessed she must be off to take that shower, so I set about feeding Hugo and cleaning things up. I was looking forward to catching up with Sam and telling her all about Rosemary and the laptop. What on earth was she so afraid was on there? It had to be more than a browsing history of Netflix box sets watched in silence to the Marriage of Figaro.

I didn't have to wait long to find out. There was a knock at the back door. The tall shadow of a man in a trench coat stood on the other side.

"Inspector Lovington, to what do I owe the honour of a visit?"

"Excuse me Reverend, I hope you don't mind my using the back door. I revisited the crime scene after interviewing Mrs Reynolds, and... I was wondering if you would be so kind as to allow me to use your phone to call HQ before heading back to my room for the night. I am very keen to find out what the IT guys have discovered on the laptop and my phone is struggling to pick up a signal."

"Inspector, of course. Would you like a drink, perhaps? The phone is on a table in the hallway. It's a rotary phone. I hope you can remember how to use them."

"I think so." *Man, that smile!* "Oh, and you have a hostess trolley. Reminds me of my mother's house. Are you expecting company? I apologise. I won't stay too long."

"Oh, just Dr Sam Hawthorne and young Dominic Creek. Freya is cooking beef bourguignon. She is becoming quite the domestic goddess."

"Sounds lovely, I am sorry, Reverend, do you mind?"

I had unconsciously followed the inspector into the hall and was standing right next to him by the table, blocking his access to the all-important phone. "Oops, sorry. Take as long as you need. I'll be in the kitchen." I scurried back and quietly prepared a salad. Tossing lettuce in a bowl with one ear open for clues. But I couldn't hear a thing. I considered testing out if the old glass-to-the-wall trick really worked.

"Well, it's always the quiet ones, isn't it?" said Inspector Lovington as he re-entered the kitchen. He sat down at the table, loosened his tie, and sighed. "I don't suppose that drink you were offering was a beer, by any chance?"

"Sorry, no beer. There is some whiskey, and I think there's an ancient bottle of Croft's Original at the back of the cupboard. It probably dates to the same year as that hostess trolley."

"A whisky on the rocks would be great, or a hot toddy before I set off out into the night."

There was that wink again!

"Inspector, if you are off duty now, would you like to stay for dinner? From the number of utensils I have just cleared away, I think my niece has cooked enough to feed an army."

"Jess, as I am off duty, I will accept your very kind offer. If I stay, though, it's on two conditions. One, you call me Dave and two, we don't discuss the case."

***

As the evening wore on, I discovered that calling him Dave was an easy condition to meet, but not discussing the case proved to be altogether more difficult. Sam had brought over even more alcoholic gifts from grateful patients (she must have a cupboard full of the stuff). And the wine, the excellent food and relaxed company ensured that the evening went by in the most agreeable manner. The more we unwound, the looser our tongues became. All of us had our theories about who killed Rachel, though the only policeman in our little group was keeping his suspicions to himself.

"I think it was her own mother." suggested Dominic. "Dr Hawthorne, you must remember, at the hospital this morning, how berserk Mrs Smith went when the doorbell rang? Scared me half to death, she did. That is not normal. Tell them, Doctor. Tell them. She was bat shit crazy!"

"It is true. Violet seems to have a problem with the doorbell, especially in the morning. But she often has stressful outbursts. The rest of the time she is extremely quiet," Sam replied.

"Except for when I found her, she wasn't very quiet then. And she was still screaming when Rosemary went in after me. And when you asked her about my father, she talked then."

"Like I said, she can be disturbed, repetitive, even loud when triggered, but most of the time, she is very subdued. Well, she has been throughout most of her stay at the hospital. Of course, that could be a reaction to the trauma of losing her daughter but... Jess, c'mon when you found her, she was on her commode! She had been there for a while and her dinner was rotting away on a tray beside her. That doesn't sound to me like someone who could strangle a fitter, younger woman. She can't even lift herself back into her bed!" Sam emphatically threw down her napkin as if it was an invitation to a duel.

Freya grabbed the opportunity to nudge her way into the conversation. "Maybe this isn't important, but I was wondering...how badly was the food decomposed? I mean, was it once breakfast? Dinner?"

"It was mouldy. How long does it take to go green? One day? Two days?" I said, curious that I had never thought about this before. I hadn't noticed what meal it was - the spread of mould made it hard to determine, and there were other things taking my attention.

Sam dived on the chance to demonstrate her scientific superiority. "With the right conditions, twelve to twenty-four hours is all it really takes. So, if Rachel died early on Friday morning, that would have been long enough. What intrigues me is that Violet Smith was on her commode. Someone or something interrupted Rachel in her care duties."

"Sam, that is my biggest puzzle too," Dave finally entered the conversation. "Rachel had taken food into her mother's room. Lifted her onto her commode and left the food on the bed tray to deal with something else and didn't return. Perhaps your theory of an intruder is correct, Jess. But why didn't they steal anything? We now know it was Rosemary who took the laptop. Nothing else appears to be missing."

"Did you find out what was on the laptop? You muttered something about it's always the quiet ones when you got off the phone." I know I had promised not to discuss the case, but as he appeared to be sharing, I thought I would push it a bit.

"I cannot discuss new evidence. Sorry, Jess... perhaps it is time for me to go. Thank you for a lovely evening. What time does the Island taxi pass by?"

As there are no cars, the taxi service is a quaint horse and cart affair. A pool of such taxis run circuits of the Island with regular stops from six in the morning through to eleven at night every day. Fortunately, the vicarage is placed so that I can access two such circuits — the last one to Market Square was due in twenty minutes.

I showed the inspector out to the stop. The night air was warmer than yesterday but was still cold enough to make the air from our breath form a mist as we spoke.

"Dave, I am sorry for pushing on the laptop. You were off duty and it's not my place to interfere."

"Jess, please don't worry. I'm really grateful for all your interest. Without you, we would never have uncovered the laptop or learnt about Rachel's chat room."

"Her chat room! What, like a live sex chat room?" I gasped.

"You certainly are not a naive medieval nun, are you? I don't want this going any further, Jess. Do you understand?" I nodded. "But, yes, it appears the bookish church mouse entertained men from her bedroom over the internet under the name Madame Mozart!"

The faint sound of horse hooves and wooden wheels approached from along the Upper Road, and we both fell into an awkward silence. I was struggling to reconcile my image of Rachel Smith with this new knowledge. No wonder Rosemary had wanted to hide the laptop. That was Rachel's online business.

"Do you think one of Madame Mozart's clients killed her?" I whispered as Dave stepped up into the cart.

"My IT people are working through her accounts. This new information increases the suspect pool considerably. It appears Madame Mozart was very popular."

And there was that wink again as the cart trotted off. I stood and waited for him to look back. But he didn't. *Jess, this isn't a Hallmark movie! Stop looking for romantic signs that just aren't there.* I took a beat to compose myself and went back inside. I returned to find Dominic and Freya playfully putting washing up bubbles on each other's noses whilst my best friend leaned elegantly back on her chair, nursing a whiskey nightcap in a short tumbler glass.

"You said the plate was covered in mould?" Sam put the drink down on the table and lifted her glasses slightly to rub her weary eyes. "A bit of mould. I understand, but the spread suggests it had been there more than a day."

"But Rachel was very much alive Friday morning. She sent me the email, remember? Perhaps she hadn't cleared away the food from the night before. She wasn't feeling well after all, and whilst she was attending to her mother on the commode, she possibly heard an intruder —"

"Hmm, I suppose so. Still, clandestine online activities, a secret trust fund, suicide, a love triangle. It's quite the mystery!" Sam tipped back the last few drops of her drink and prepared ready to leave.

"Suicide?" I asked.

"Yes, Jess, your father. Remember Violet Smith said he jumped."

"Yes, yes, she did. But she lied to her own daughter for forty years. Not sure I would put much stock in anything that woman says." Despite all the revelations of the last few days, I wasn't prepared to think about the possibility of my father ending his own life.

"True, maybe she has convinced herself he jumped... though, surely to believe it was an accident would be easier. Anyway, whatever happened, it was a long time ago and we will never know the truth, will we? Best not to dwell on it. I'm sorry to have mentioned it. I'd better get going. I'm on earlies tomorrow... Freya, sweetheart, that beef thing was delightful, as are you. And Dominic, be careful with ladders from now on, please. You two make the cutest couple! I'll let myself out." And with a kiss on both their cheeks and a dramatic wave in my direction, my best friend swept out into the frozen night — remarkably steady on her feet considering how much alcohol she had drunk.

I left the cutest couple in Wesberrey to finish the dishes and retired to my bed. Sam was right. There was no way of knowing what happened on that cliff forty years ago. Knowing if my father fell, jumped or was pushed, would not bring him back or change the past four decades. As my Aunt Cindy would say, some things are best left to rest. Rachel's murder, though, was current and her killer was still at large. If it was one of Madame Mozart's clients, then he could have killed or would kill other women. The very thought sent a chill down my spine.

Anyone could be one of her clients? What about Hugh Burton? Had he recognised Madame Mozart when he visited Rachel earlier in the week? Maybe Arabella had asked him to have a chat with Rachel and when he got there, he realised who she was? Could Rachel have identified him? I don't think the host can see those calling in, but she might have known him by his voice. The potential scandal for someone in Hugh's position would be career changing. Did he sneak back on Friday morning and strangle her? The irony was that Rachel would have been one of the few people who wouldn't have known who Hugh was, as she didn't own a TV set unless she watched it online? But then he had been having an affair with a married socialite for decades. Would a little online perversion really threaten him that much? What if Arabella found out? Did she kill her half-sister in a jealous rage or to silence her forever?

The wine and the questions swam around my head as I drifted off to the soft farewells of young lovers on the vicarage doorstep and the hum of a distant scooter. As Scarlett O'Hara said, 'Tomorrow is another day.'

The Devil Takes his Own

T he phone downstairs woke me from my slumbers. Knowing it would soon click over to the answerphone, I rolled back over and snuggled back down into my pillow. My peace, though, was only temporary. The voice recording afterwards echoed loud. Its message so disturbing that the words bounded up the stairs and kicked me out of my warm bed.

"Jess! It's me, Sam... You might want to stop by the hospital on your rounds? Violet Smith is dead."

It transpired that Violet had died in her sleep in the early hours of the morning, one week after the death of her daughter. I called my mother and told her she need not be afraid of Violet Smith anymore. I advised her I would go to the hospital to offer prayers of comfort to the staff and patients, nothing more. Despite all I had heard over the past few days about Violet Smith, I still felt sad for her passing away, heartbroken and alone, on a stark hospital ward with no one to mourn her.

"Best way to go, if yer ask me, Reverend. Slip quietly away. No crocodile tears. No dramatics. Some folks would say it's a sad end, but can there be a happy one? Hmmpf, can't be nice to see everyone yer love gathered around yer bed just waiting for yer to breathe yer last." Martha shook her head and sucked her teeth to emphasise her point. "Hear them a-weeping and a-wailing! No, Reverend, that there's how I want to die. Just fall asleep and let the good Lord take me home without any fuss and nonsense."

"You appear to have given it a lot of thought." I had not had the chance to talk properly to Martha before. Admittedly, the first and last time we met, I had just come from a murder scene and wasn't in the mood for small talk and other such pleasantries. And I could barely breathe.

"This place gives me plenty of time to think, especially about death. Of course, back home, we would now be arranging the Dead Yard to celebrate her life and an end to her troubles."

"I am sorry, what is a Dead Yard?" I asked.

"It's a wonderful Caribbean tradition, especially back in Kingston. The rum flows for nine nights of mourning. There be food, music. Man, yer spirit be in no rush to cross over with all that going on! Let the living say their goodbyes in their own way and yer listen from afar. No need to be beating yer breast." Martha's mahogany eyes sparkled with the recollections of her home traditions. Sam said that it was really Martha Campbell who ran the hospital, and she would be in chaos without her. I could see why Sam valued her work so highly. In the time the hospital's receptionist had been speaking to me, she had opened and sorted a pile of letters, entered an appointment on the computer and was now tidying up the magazines in the waiting area. "Poor Miss Smith, I doubt there will be anyone drinking rum in her memory or beating their breasts over her passing."

My mother is probably drinking a glass of something in celebration.

"Place be a lot quieter though. That lady had a set of lungs on her when she got going. No need for a cockerel with Miss Smith raising all the chickens in the coup!" Martha laughed with her whole body. Her upper arms and huge bosom jiggled in perfect harmony.

It was then I realised I had never rung the doorbell. I had been here twice, and, on both occasions, I had just strolled in through the sliding doors.

"Martha, is there a doorbell here?"

"Yes, at the side, hardly anyone uses it. It's for tradesmen and deliveries outside of general opening hours. Sometimes out of hours for emergencies. Why d'yer ask?"

"Just something my young friend Dominic said about Miss Smith being agitated when the doorbell rang... Martha, what time does the post normally get here?"

"Mr Barrett always make me his first stop. He gets the seven-thirty ferry, so usually about eight o'clock."

"And does he ring the doorbell?"

"Of course, we don't open till eight-thirty. There is always a queue for the day clinic, which starts at nine o'clock prompt."

"And last Friday, was he here at eight am?"

"Of course. I remember him asking the time because he'd left his phone at home. People get so attached to those blessed tings, whatever did we do before, eh?" She tutted and rolled her eyes. "At least me watch is strapped on tight to me wrist. Said the same to him. Funny ting, last week, he actually stopped to help me with the chairs for the clinic."

"Does he do that often?"

Martha laughed again. "No, never! Man's always rushing, barely has time to say hello. I told him he needs to slow down, enjoy the view! So, Reverend Ward, is there anything else I can help yer with?"

"No, thank you, Martha, you have been most helpful!"

Tangled Web

My gut was telling me that Robert Barrett was Rachel's murderer, and yet I couldn't work it out. He must have given Rachel a lift home on Thursday, after I left, to collect her copy of Divine Love and then later brought it over with the wallpaper. Obviously, he knew Rachel was coming to help me with the decorating and that explained how he knew there would be no books to collect from Island Books on Friday afternoon. Martha had just confirmed that Robert was at the hospital when Rachel sent the email. But something about his response to Inspector Lovington made me suspicious. After all, he denied having any personal relationship with her, and that was clearly untrue. I suppose he could have popped over to the Smith's house, after helping Martha with the chairs, thinking it was empty? My biggest question was why? What was his motive? He was an odious pig of a man and downright menacing, but that doesn't make him a thief or a murderer. Robert's words about it being a 'business arrangement' were pinging inside my brain like a pinball. I knew that there was something I was missing. Violet's reaction to the doorbell was bugging me as well. Maybe it was just a random trigger for her and she had a phobia of doorbells, or maybe, as I suspected, it was the connection with the man ringing the bell.

Whilst I was certain that Rosemary and Lord Somerstone were innocent, I couldn't ignore the possibility that either Arabella or Hugh were guilty. I had no evidence to prove in their favour either way.

I took my time strolling back to the Vicarage. The crisp morning air was slapping my thoughts into shape as I walked. I arrived to find a very distraught niece handing me the hall phone.

"It's Aunt Cindy. She says she needs to speak to you. Urgently." Freya anxiously bit the corner of her lip as I took the phone.

"Cindy, what's up? Are you ok? Freya looks very troubled. Are you hurt? Mum? Aunt Pam? Are they ok?"

The familiar voice on the other end was surprisingly calm, given Freya's demeanour.

"Now Jess, darling, I need you to listen to me very carefully. I want you to promise to put your normal scepticism aside and do what I tell you. Do you understand?"

I looked quizzically at my niece, whose eyes implored me to listen to what my aunt had to say. "Okay?" I said.

"Darling, I want you to promise."

"Okay, I promise. Now, please, I am very busy."

"Yes, I know you are. Very busy uncovering murderers and getting yourself into a whole heap of trouble. I know that you have worked it out, or you will do shortly. You will want to act upon your suspicions but please Jess, and I cannot state this any clearer. Whatever you do, do not go near the water. Promise me. You will stay away from any water."

"Water? What are you talking about? I have no idea who killed Rachel." Which was true. All I had were suspicions but even if I did, how could Cindy possibly know that? Freya's concern was obvious/ My crazy hippie aunt had told her I was in danger. I had had enough of this.

"Aunt, if I promise to stay away from water for the rest of the day, will you promise me you will stop putting this stupid psychic mumbo jumbo into my niece's head? We both know there is no earthly way you can know what is going on in my mind, nor can you predict anything in the future. You are scaring Freya and frustrating me. Now, if you don't mind,

Barbara is patiently waiting for me in my office to write up the parish newsletter. Is there anything else?"

"Jessamy, I will do whatever I can to keep you safe, but my influence is useless if you deliberately put yourself in harm's way. Please... just be careful. I love you both."

Her influence? What utter nonsense! I put down the receiver and looked up, just in time to see Freya's exasperated face turn away as she ran to her room. Within seconds, the phone rang again. I snatched it up.

"Aunt Cindy, please, I need to get on with my work!"

"Reverend Ward? Is that you? I am sorry I must have dialled incorrectly." This voice had a very different timbre, and I recognised its deep tones straight away.

"Excuse me, Inspector Lovington? My apologies, I thought it was someone else. How may I help you?"

"Reverend, I have just left the coroner's office and, whilst this is not strictly protocol, I thought you might be interested to hear that we have been wrong about the time of death. Rachel was murdered on Thursday, not Friday, which explains the rotting food."

"Thursday? So, who sent the email?"

The room was spinning. I tried and failed to grab the hallway table. My palm slipped off the side and I dropped the receiver. Pulling the stretchy cord back up with one hand, I tried to steady myself with the other.

"Exactly, Reverend, can you corroborate Rosemary Reynolds' statement that the laptop was in Rachel's bedroom when you found her?"

"Sorry, Inspector, I can't remember. I was so shocked to see Rachel lying there... You cannot seriously suspect Rosemary?" It has to be Robert Barrett, but how? I could not explain the email. He was putting out chairs in the hospital when it was sent.

"I'm coming back on the next ferry and will ask PC Taylor to bring Mrs Reynolds down to the incident room. If you remember anything, please call me straight away. Good day, Reverend."

I turned around to see Barbara standing at the foot of the stairs, holding out a cup of tea. "I am sorry, Vicar. I didn't mean to eavesdrop but, I thought you might need a pick-me-up."

"Yes, thank you. That is most kind. Shall we go into my office? This newsletter won't write itself now, will it?" I followed Barbara, and we sat silently facing each other across the desk for several minutes.

"Vicar, did I hear you correctly? Do the police think old Rosemary did it? That woman was more like a mother to that poor girl than ever her real mother was." Barbara stared out of the office window in the direction of Love Lane. "I can't believe it, Vicar. There has to be another explanation."

"I feel they are making a mistake too, Barbara. But if Rachel died on Thursday, who else could have sent the email to me on Friday morning? Oh, my goodness, the poor woman was already dead!" The reality hit me hard. To think that no one knew until I found Rachel's body on Saturday morning. Violet had been stuck on that commode for nearly two days! No wonder she was hysterical when I found her. "It must have been Rosemary. She must have learnt that Rachel was coming to help me. She felt betrayed after all the years she has loved and supported her and in a jealous rage, she strangled her. Then she went back the next morning and sent the email to cover her tracks."

"Then why take the laptop? And why hand it over to you later? Rosemary was so upset. She was telling me and Phil yesterday how ashamed she was having the police in her house. It doesn't make sense." Barbara ran her fingers through her cropped, bleached hair and sighed deeply. "And to be honest, Vicar, I can't see old Rosemary being a whiz at IT. I don't see her as one of them silver surfers, do you?"

"Not really, no... but if it wasn't Rosemary... who? It had to be someone who knew Rachel was coming here, but why send the email at all? Surely it was a huge risk to return to the murder scene just to send a message?"

Barbara was obviously enjoying playing detective. "Maybe they didn't leave the house at all?"

"Hmmm, but surely Violet's screams would have either driven them away or —"

"The murderer would have silenced her!" Barbara's hand shot up to cover her open mouth. "Violet can't have known who the murderer was... if she had seen them, then surely they would have killed her too."

"Or maybe she saw them, but they didn't see her? Bah, there is no way that she would have remained silent all night. By the morning she must have been so agitated. Especially if she heard someone re-entering the house..." I was also thinking about her reaction to the doorbell, but surely the murderer wouldn't be stupid enough to ring.

"So the killer didn't see her." Barbara stood up and paced up and down the oriental carpet in front of the desk. Taking off both of her earrings, she started to throw and catch them in one hand as she walked and talked through all the possible scenarios, dismissing them one by one. "What if..." Barbara spun around, indicating that she was experiencing an eureka moment. "What if the killer scheduled the email to go out later? And then left. They could then go away and create for themselves a perfect alibi for the time of the email."

"Barbara Graham, you are a genius! Call Phil and tell him to ensure that Bob McGuire takes the ferry out to meet the Inspector straight away, unless it's already out, of course. And then call PC Taylor and convince him to get to the harbour as soon as possible. Robert Barrett must not leave the Island. I will meet them all by the ferry."

Stay Away from the Water

I had felt it. If I was being honest, I had felt it from the outset. I had felt it was Robert. He was the only person who knew that Rachel was coming to help me with the decorating on Friday morning. I was right that Rachel seemed agitated about him, but maybe that agitation was fear, not lust. The business agreement must have been something to do with Rachel's online activities. He mentioned the 'man in black' Was that to throw me off the scent or did he think Hugh was also one of her clients? Did he kill her in a jealous rage? Did she refuse his advances, or was it a sex game that went badly wrong?

Whatever the motive, he was cunning enough to hack her laptop to schedule the email and ensure that he had a cast iron alibi for the time it was sent. Not only that, but he was calculating enough to leave the laptop behind. Most people would have panicked and taken it with them. Surely the police would find he was one of her clients. That was risky unless he knew his account was untraceable. So devious! He must have strangled her, scheduled the email and then nonchalantly continued to bring me the book and the wallpaper as if nothing had happened.

I reached the Cliff station but there was no sign of Tom or Ernest. I checked my watch. They must be having lunch. I marched to the White House and beat as hard as I could on their front door. A surprised Tom opened the door, gently dabbing his mouth with a white cotton napkin.

138

"Tom, sorry to disturb you, but I know who killed Rachel and I have to get down to the ferry immediately. We have to stop him from leaving the Island before the Inspector returns!"

"Reverend Ward, of course. Ernest put your best running shoes on. Duty calls!"

Within minutes, the two men were cranking the old railway back into life and we were descending to the harbour station at top speed. On the way down, I explained to them both everything I knew.

"Madame Mozart, eh?" Tom was almost salivating over this latest piece of hot gossip. "you say that the Inspector said she had quite the client list... Well, well, it all goes on here at Wesberrey, eh? I wonder what Rachel's unique selling point was. They always have a 'trick', don't they? A thing that is distinctively theirs to draw in the punters. Oooh, do you think she acted as a librarian... a secretary...music teacher? Or a naughty headmistress!"

Ernest was not amused. "Tom! Enough! Rachel was our friend and fellow PCC member, and Lord Somerstone's daughter. There is no need to further besmirch her good name with idle chit-chat. What she did in the privacy of her own home was her business. Reverend Ward, once we have her murderer in custody, we must do all we can to maintain Miss Smith's reputation, don't you agree?"

"Ernest, I do. But I fear everything will come out at trial. This will be a juicy story for the tabloids, but we will do what we can. First, let's get her killer behind bars!"

The moment the carriage landed, Ernest pulled open the metal doors, and we all ran towards the jetty where a small crowd was already beginning to gather. Phil waved at me from across the square and jogged over.

"Got Barbara's message, Vicar. Sent McGuire out to fetch the Inspector and PC Taylor is on 'is way down. They were en route to arrest Rosemary Reynolds. What bloody nonsense! The postie 'as not left yet, and 'e can't now, without getting past us. I got a few lads from the pub to come out as back-up. Nothing as cunnin' as a cornered animal in my experience. Bob left me some rope to tie the bastard up when we get 'im." Phil proudly showed off the battered blue rope and pointed to the far right corner of Market Square.

139

"I reckon 'e'll come down the back end of Lower Road, that's 'is usual route. Stan is on look-out. We've got the whole town involved. Mr Barrett won't get away."

Minutes later, the frantic sound of a tinkling bicycle bell interrupted the general mumble of excited onlookers, as Stan Matthews's teenage son hurtled across the cobbled square toward us.

"Dad says he's here!"

Phil marshalled everyone around to the side of the pub. "We must let 'im get out of the van first. If 'e suspects somethin', 'e'll be off like a whippet out of the traps."

The Royal Mail van pulled up by the side of the jetty, and Robert sat in the cabin, writing notes on his clipboard. Phil motioned for everyone to encircle the Ape. We all edged our way carefully across to create a wall between him and the Square.

Fortunately, Robert was concentrating so intensely on his paperwork that he didn't notice. When the last of our motley crew was in place, I walked up to the harbour side of the van and knocked on the window.

"Hello Robert, I was just waiting for the ferry. Have you finished your rounds for the day?"

He looked up, distracted. "Why, Vicar. Fancy meeting you here. Heading back to the mainland, eh? Not enough souls for you to save on Wesberrey, then."

"Can't save a person's soul, only they can do that. I am not a Catholic priest. I can't absolve you from sin, but I am willing to hear your confession." My heart was pounding so violently that I was sure he could see it through my cleric's shirt.

Robert opened the cabin door and stepped out towards me, slamming the metallic door shut. "And what makes you think I have anything to confess?" he snarled.

"Why did you kill her? Did you mean to do it or was it an accident? It was very clever of you to schedule the ema-"

Robert grabbed the front of my shirt with both hands and pulled my torso towards him. I could feel his hot breath invading my own and his stubbled chin hovered within grazing distance of my face.

"She was a proper minx, that one, a right little tease. Doing all that stuff on the internet, but when it came to pleasing a real man, she was a frightened little rabbit. I dare say you have more game in you, despite that dog collar. I only wanted to try the goods for real. She acted so coy, but finally agreed. Then you showed up. Her bloody sister - a priest! She promised, you see, so we went up to her house with the wallpaper to get that bloody book for you. She invited me in, but then kept me waiting for ages. Downstairs in that kitchen. Not much of a hostess. I mean, she didn't even have any coffee. So I followed her upstairs. Caught her on the landing. She ushered me into her room. I recognised it from her 'Madame Mozart' calls. Hmm, brought back some very good memories. I was raring to go, but she asked me to be patient, that she had to sort something out first. Really, who the hell did she think she was, eh? I had bloody waited long enough."

"So you killed her?"

"Technically, yes. I didn't mean to but you see... Madame Mozart plays the submissive so I expected her to be quiet but she didn't make a sound! Silly bitch didn't cry out or anything. That minx let me tighten the scarf around her scrawny neck and didn't even try to stop me. Then she just went all limp." Robert increased his hold on my shirt and started to pull me back towards the van.

"You won't get away with it!" I protested as I tried to break free.

"Perhaps. But I am sure you understand that I have to try. Now, if you'll be so kind as to step into the Ape, we can leave on the next ferry. It should be here any minute. I suggest you be like Rachel and go quietly." Robert pushed me against the van.

I heard Phil's voice yelling "Charge!" and the cries of an angry mob crashed over us. Robert stumbled and swung me around.

"You are a right piece of work, eh, Vicar!"

I felt a sudden punch to my stomach and a violent shove. The shock made me lose my breath and my footing. I hadn't realised how close I was to the end of the quay and, before I could call out, I was thundering down below the waterline. It was cold - unlike anything I had ever felt before. The air was sucked from my lungs. I fell deeper and deeper. Rough waves buffeted me against the concrete harbour wall. I reached out to the lifebuoys strung around the edge, grabbed hold of the orange rope that held them fast and pulled myself along the side. Finally, I reached the jetty ladder. My hands were numb. I couldn't breathe. The rungs were rusty and brittle, but somehow, I slowly pulled myself up to the top, and then everything went dark.

Flowers and Bed Gowns

"Now Jess, you need to get some rest. Doctor's orders. Freya is bringing over a change of clothes - seems the choice is black, navy, or grey. Don't you even have any fun cardies?" My best friend was busily plumping my pillows as she spoke.

"No, Sam, I do not. I hate cardigans. Anyway, do you wear cardigans at work? Hmm? That said, anything is better than this hospital gown. Where are my other clothes?"

"Oh, you mean the sombre black ensemble you went for a midday swim in. I wanted to put them in the incinerator, but Martha is getting them laundered for you."

"Will you thank her for me? How did I get here? I don't remember anything after climbing up the harbour ladder."

"Of course not, Jess. You were unconscious. You are very brave, quite the hero I hear, but my main concern is that you are most definitely suffering from shock and probably hypothermia. My dear, you are very lucky not to be dead. We will toast your valour later, but for now, you need to rest and stay warm. I will come around later to check on you. Oh, and Inspector Loveliness popped by whilst you were out cold. Don't worry, I wouldn't let him see you in this get-up. But he will be back later. Don't you at least have a pretty nightdress Freya could bring?"

"I wear old t-shirts most of the time... and stop it. I am sure he is only here to get my statement."

"Hmm, well, doesn't mean you can't make an effort." Sam bent down to kiss me on the forehead. "See you in about an hour. If you need anything, just press the orange button."

I must have fallen back asleep. The next thing I remember was waking to a fuzzy sea of colourful blooms dancing before my eyes. "Don't all crowd her at once. She's been through so much already, the poor dear..." Barbara ordered everyone into an orderly line.

"We've cleaned out the flower stall in Market Square. I'm not sure the 'ospital has enough vases. Barbara and I'll go over to the vestry and bring a few over later. You 'ad us all worried sick, Vicar." Phil sat down on the side of my bed and laid his bunch of carnations on my stomach.

"They are lovely, thank you. Thank all of you. Did we get him?"

"Oh yes indeed, Vicar. What a show! Phil and Ernest rugby tackled that horrid man to the ground. They were both so brave and strong." Tom gazed admiringly at his courageous partner. One by one, they retold their part in the capture, and like any good fisherman's tale, their stories got larger and larger.

From behind the back of this small crowd, Rosemary slowly stepped forward, walked around to the other side of my bed and sat hunched in the blue straight-backed chair on my left side.

"Reverend, thank you so very much for finding Rachel's killer and ..." she sobbed, "and for believing in me. I'm not sure this old ticker would have stood a night in a police cell."

I took her hand and smiled.

"It was a team effort. Barbara here worked out how he sent the email. That's what sealed it. I couldn't have done it without you. Without any of you." Never had my heart been so close to bursting with love and pride as it did at that moment. I have never married or had children. I have been proud of my own achievements, of course, but I realised nothing is as powerful as a vicarious pride in the successful efforts of others. "Shall we take a moment to pray?"

"That is a wonderful idea Reverend," said Ernest, and we all held hands as I spoke a warmly felt prayer of gratitude. As we finished, there was a gentle knock on the door and a polite cough followed. "Excuse me, Reverend, but may I take your statement now?"

There really was something about that man's hair and fluorescent lighting. He looked like an angel. "Certainly, Inspector. Please come in."

I straightened my bed covers and tried to position the flowers to stop them from falling as Phil got off the bed to leave. The Inspector bowed to each member of the PCC as they filed past him into the hallway.

"I am relieved to see you sitting up and looking so well. You had quite the ordeal, Reverend Ward."

"Yes, if I had thought it through a bit better, I would have been more careful, but..."

"You were very brave — if a little foolhardy. Next time, leave it to the professionals, okay?"

"Oh, there won't be a next time. Believe me." I desperately wanted the inspector to sit beside me, as Phil had done, but he remained a safe distance away at the foot of the bed.

"Well, that's good to hear. And thank you. You solved the case. The murderer is safely behind bars in Stourchester Prison. I will take your statement tomorrow. There's no rush. I only wanted to say that it has been a pleasure working with you, Reverend Ward."

"So, you'll be leaving us?" I knew he would be once he'd solved the case. His job was in the crime centre that is Stourchester, not the sleepy isle that is Wesberrey.

"I am sure we will meet again, Jess. In fact, Cynthia has said I will be back here very soon indeed." *There, he winked again!*

"Ah yes, my Aunt Cindy and her fortune telling. Do you know she warned me to keep away from water?" Maybe I should have listened.

Departures and Arrivals

T he next few days passed by quietly. Inspector Lovington came back, as promised, but this time with PC Taylor to take down my official statement. There were no winks, and he did not call me Jess. I told myself that was probably just as well. I was way too old and far too busy for any silly flirtations.

Sam discharged me into the care of my niece, who had notified her university tutor that she would be back a few weeks later than planned, as she needed to nurse her courageous aunt. I know that the delayed return to her studies had more to do with eeking out more precious time with a certain young man than an actual need to sit at my bedside. Unfortunately, all this subterfuge was in vain as Dominic had to return to university early to re-sit an exam. In truth, despite, or possibly because of her Pre-Raphaelite charms, I think he found Freya more of a dangerous distraction than an inspirational muse.

So it was that on this freakishly warm sunny day at the tail end of January we gathered at the Cat and Fiddle to wish Dominic au revoir. Cindy had persuaded my other aunt, Pamela, and her husband, Byron, to join us. The two sisters could not be more different. Where Cindy was youthful and charming, a lilac and silver vision, Pamela was old and settled, a thin, leathery woman dressed in a colour I can only describe as mud brown. Byron was a slight man whose greyness of eyes and hair matched his suit so well he was almost invisible. They sat at the end of the table together and barely spoke two words to each other, or to anyone else, for the length of the meal.

Still, it was good to meet them again, and it was an immeasurable joy to have my old and new family around me. Phil put on a lovely spread and joined us for dessert. Barbara had baked a delicious carrot cake and Rosemary, Tom, Ernest, Sam and Martha all had a seat at our table. After the craziness of the past few weeks, it was wonderful to join as one to eat good food and drink fine wine. I led us all in a short prayer of gratitude for the bounty we had enjoyed and the company we shared. The clock on the Guildhall counted down the seconds and it was soon time for Dominic to go. He and Freya slipped out to say their farewells on the quayside.

With a few minutes to spare before the ferry departed, the rest of the party strolled down to the water's edge to wave our young friend goodbye. The ferry docked, and the stern opened to set down its inward passengers. Freya sauntered back to join us as Dominic waited to embark.

"It's okay Freya, you will see him again soon. You are both coming to stay for Easter. You will be so busy here with the plans for my installation, the time will fly by." I tried to comfort my niece, though I knew my words were falling short.

Freya waved at Dominic as he disappeared onboard. "I know Aunt Jess. it's just... he just... he just told me he loves me!"

"Oh! And?" I asked, "What did you reply?"

"I said I love him, too!"

I threw my arms around my niece and squeezed her as tightly as I could. "Ah, Freya, I am so happy for you. He is a lovely young man."

"Who's a lovely young man?" It was a voice I had known all my life.

"Zuzu? What are you doing here?"

"Mum?" Freya turned around, obviously as stunned as I was.

"Surprise! Frey-Frey, come here, right now, and give your mother a great big hug. Oh, it's so wonderful to be here. Look at us three, all back home on Wesberrey. We'll have such fun! Jessie, I trust there's room in that big old vicarage for little ole me. I might be staying a while!"

The End

What's Next for Jessame?
MAUSOLEUM MADNESS

Wrong Doers, it's time to say your prayers! Jess Ward has only been back on the Isle of Wesberrey for a few weeks, but all the recent drama has made it feel a lot longer. Drama much increased by the unexpected arrival of her sister Susannah. The bishop is due in a few days to formally install her into the benefice of St. Bridget's and there is so much to prepare. Add to that a double funeral and a surprise visit from her mother and Jess has no time for family legends about the 'godmother' and the Well of the Triple Goddess. However, the disappearance of a wealthy businessman forces Jess to re-examine her personal connection to this ancient family myth - her family claim they can sense that he is dead. It's all madness, of course. But the discovery of his body at his father-in-law's funeral drags them all back into the island's darkest secrets. Her best friend has gone AWOL with the handsome undertaker and her sister is proving to be an unwanted distraction for the dishy police inspector. Things move fast on Wesberrey, and it's enough to make Jess dizzy. Or is that the result of reconnecting with her pagan past?

PENELOPE CRESS
STEVE HIGGS

GREENFIELD
PRESS

MAUSOLEUM
MADNESS

More Books By Steve Higgs

Blue Moon Investigations
Paranormal Nonsense
The Phantom of Barker Mill
Amanda Harper Paranormal Detective
The Klowns of Kent
Dead Pirates of Cawsand
In the Doodoo With Voodoo
The Witches of East Malling
Crop Circles, Cows and Crazy Aliens
Whispers in the Rigging
Bloodlust Blonde – a short story
Paws of the Yeti
Under a Blue Moon – A Paranormal
Detective Origin Story
Night Work
Lord Hale's Monster
The Herne Bay Howlers
Undead Incorporated
The Ghoul of Christmas Past
The Sandman
Jailhouse Golem
Shadow in the Mine

Felicity Philips Investigates
To Love and to Perish
Tying the Noose
Aisle Kill Him
A Dress to Die For

Patricia Fisher Cruise Mysteries
The Missing Sapphire of Zangrabar
The Kidnapped Bride
The Director's Cut
The Couple in Cabin 2124
Doctor Death
Murder on the Dancefloor
Mission for the Maharaja
A Sleuth and her Dachshund in Athens
The Maltese Parrot
No Place Like Home

Patricia Fisher Mystery Adventures
What Sam Knew
Solstice Goat
Recipe for Murder
A Banshee and a Bookshop
Diamonds, Dinner Jackets, and Death
Frozen Vengeance
Mug Shot
The Godmother
Murder is an Artform
Wonderful Weddings and Deadly
Divorces
Dangerous Creatures

Patricia Fisher: Ship's Detective Series
The Ship's Detective
Fitness Can Kill
Death by Pirates

Albert Smith Culinary Capers
Pork Pie Pandemonium
Bakewell Tart Bludgeoning
Stilton Slaughter
Bedfordshire Clanger Calamity
Death of a Yorkshire Pudding
Cumberland Sausage Shocker
Arbroath Smokie Slaying
Dundee Cake Dispatch
Lancashire Hotpot Peril
Blackpool Rock Bloodshed
Kent Coast Oyster Obliteration

Realm of False Gods
Untethered magic
Unleashed Magic
Early Shift
Damaged but Powerful
Demon Bound
Familiar Territory
The Armour of God
Live and Die by Magic
Terrible Secrets

Printed in Great Britain
by Amazon

22742645R00086